THYRA

STEVEN GRIER WILLIAMS

9/30/22

To Sarah !!

Thank you for the support !!

I hope you enjoy !!

Also it was great meeting you !!

MILFORD HOUSE

an imprint of Sunbury Press, Inc.
Mechanicsburg, PA USA

MILFORD
HOUSE

an imprint of Sunbury Press, Inc.
Mechanicsburg, PA USA

For information about special discounts for bulk purchases, please contact Sunbury Press Orders Dept. at (855) 338-8359 or orders@sunburypress.com.

To request one of our authors for speaking engagements or book signings, please contact Sunbury Press Publicity Dept. at publicity@sunburypress.com.

FIRST MILFORD HOUSE PRESS EDITION: August 2022

Set in Adobe Garamond | Interior design by Crystal Devine | Cover by Derek Thornton/Notch Design | Edited by Abigail Henson.

Publisher's Cataloging-in-Publication Data
Names: Williams, Steven Grier, author.
Title: Thyra / Steven Grier Williams.
Description: First trade paperback edition. | Mechanicsburg, PA : Milford House Press, 2022.
Summary: Long ago, a powerful creature committed genocide against the dark elves of Svartalfheim. One family escaped to Midgard. Years later, Thyra, the child of the escaped family, is visited by three malevolent Valkyries and forced on a journey where she must face her past, present, and future, while fighting to save the lives of her marginalized race.
Identifiers: ISBN : 978-1-62006-954-7 (softcover).
Subjects: Fantasy | FICTION / Fantasy / Action & Adventure | FICTION / Fairy Tales, Folk Tales, Legends & Mythology.

Product of the United States of America
0 1 1 2 3 5 8 13 21 34 55

Continue the Enlightenment!

This book is dedicated to Gail McDermott.
She was kind and patient. Without her taking a chance on me,
I would not be where I am today. Rest in peace Gail.

ACKNOWLEDGMENTS

I would like to thank everyone who read my second novel and provided such wonderful and helpful feedback. I love you all!

PROLOGUE

"We had a life in Svartalfheim, but thanks to Odin's senseless war, that is over," said Ase as she helped her husband pull their boat ashore. "Why is it when he acts, we all suffer?"

Hagen grabbed the rope sitting at the front of the craft and wrapped it around a massive tree trunk before tying it tightly. He looked at his wife, who adjusted the boat a tiny bit more on the beach.

"The Allfather is not the god we thought he was," said Hagen. "Nor is his brutish son. But we can make a new home here. There are few dark elves in Midgard. We won't be found here."

Ase let go of the boat and looked at her surroundings. Above her was a starry sky with a full moon. Behind her was an expansive sea and a dense forest in front of her.

"Midgard," she whispered. "The realm of man. Humans are different from us. Their lives are short, and their physiology is fragile. We won't fit in here."

"You forgot to mention humans can be dangerous too. Their short lives make them immature, and their fragility forces them to act in groups, compensating for their lack of individual strength. But Midgard is the only place we can go mostly undetected," said Hagen. "Like it or not, this is our home now, and it is relatively safe."

"Until the Valkyries show up."

"That's not for hundreds of years, and we'll deal with that when the time comes."

"It doesn't seem like you two like it here all that much," said a man stepping out of the forest.

Immediately, Ase and Hagen drew swords.

The man raised his hand and said, "Easy. I do not mean either of you any harm. I heard you talking. I've never met a dark elf before."

Hagen cautiously stepped between the man and his wife.

"Who are you, and what do you want?" he asked.

The man spun around one time. He was unarmed as far as Ase and Hagen could tell. He proceeded to step forward cautiously.

"My name is Erlend," he said. "I live here on this island with my family. You are not going to find enemies of dark elves here. We heard about what happened to your people . . . we know loss too."

"Word has already spread this far?" said Hagen.

Erlend nodded.

"You say you know loss? What of it?" asked Ase.

"Have you heard what happened at Nyköping? It was a human town," said Erlend.

Ase nodded.

"It was our home until about a year ago when the gods came," said Erlend.

Ase hung her head.

"That was a great tragedy," she whispered.

There was a silence between the three adults, and a breeze swept in from the sea.

"Dinner is being prepared at our farm. You two should come join us," said Erlend. "We can relish in our misery of loss together . . . as a family."

Hagen and Ase looked at one another with caution in their eyes.

"It's not a trap," said Erlend. "Well, you may think it is when you taste the quality of the food. But we have plenty of mead to wash away any bad taste."

Hagen and Ase's skepticism remained.

"We can't spend our life in Midgard alone," whispered Ase.

"Weren't you the one who just noted that we would not fit in here?" Hagen said.

"And you said humans are dangerous. . . . I'm trying to be open-minded."

"Humans are dangerous. No one knows that better than other humans, which is why we live on this island," said Erlend.

Ase and Hagen looked at one another.

"We'll stay for one drink," said Hagen to Erlend.

"Fantastic. Come, I'll lead the way."

One Hundred and Seventy-four Years Later

"And that, Calder, is how we met your great, great, great, great, great grandfather. He was right about the food being bad, but the mead was amazing. Hence your family's bustling mead export to halls all over Midgard," said Ase, sitting across from the young man, who was listening intently.

"That's amazing," said Calder. "You two carry with you so much history."

"We've known every generation of your family for the past two centuries. Elves have lifespans that can last for hundreds of years. Right now, we would be the equivalent of roughly thirty in a human lifespan. Our bodies age quickly as children, just like humans, but once we reach adulthood, our aging slows to an extreme crawl. If nothing happens to us, we will be telling your great, great, great, great, great-grandson about you one day," said Hagen.

"Incredible," Calder said. "Just incredible."

"But now, for the reason we wanted to sit you down, Calder. We have exciting news to share . . . for the first time, your family will get to help raise the next generation of ours," said Ase.

"You're pregnant?" said Calder, his eyes lighting up.

"I am," Ase said.

Calder's mouth dropped open in surprise and elation. He looked at Ase, then at Hagen, then back at Ase.

"I can't believe it. I'm so happy for you two. This is so exciting. Finally, a new Olufgullveig. Not that the old Olufgullveigs are not great, but a baby dark elf. I can't wait. Have you told my parents and sister?" said Calder.

"We told them as soon as we found out, but you were still at sea," said Hagen.

"This is such good news," Calder said. "I'm so happy for you."

Nine Months Later

"Mom grab towels," shouted Erika.

"Is there anything I can do?" said Hagen.

"Get water. Plenty of it," she said.

"What about me?" said Calder.

"Go, help mom," said Erika.

"Calder, where are the buckets?" said Hagen in a panic.

Calder paused, not able to think straight.

"Calder," said Hagen.

"Over there, by the hjell."

"Ase, breathe deep now. Steady," said Erika. "Here we go."

Eight Hours Later

Erika entered the room where Ase rested against a few pillows, and Hagen sat next to her in an old wooden chair. Candles burned all around them. Their attention shifted away from each other and towards Erika as soon as she entered.

"Hello, new mom and dad," said Erika as she approached with a swaddled baby.

She passed the child to Ase, who took the baby into her arms. Hagen hovered over Ase and their child.

"Have you thought of a name?" Erika said.

"We have," said Ase looking into their baby's eyes. "Her name is Thyra."

A CRACKED HULL

Present—Twenty-five Years Later

Waves crashed upon the starboard side of the small, karvi longship as it passed through a storm that cropped up out of nowhere. Heavy droplets of rain landed on the deck and washed over the faces of the two brave crew members struggling against the powerful sea. Wood strained, ropes stretched, and muscles burned.

"We've survived worse than this. Just keep rowing," shouted Calder.

"All this for some mead," shouted Thyra, who rowed with all the might her body permitted her.

Sea spray blasted the deck, mixing with the rain, soaking the two sailors.

"It's not just mead," said Calder. "It's our mead."

He then laughed as another wave crashed against the longship.

"I see the storm breaking," shouted Thyra as the clouds ahead began to part.

"See, . . . I knew we'd be fine," said Calder.

Just then, a loud crack caught the attention of the two, and they looked at the starboard side of the longship—water was rushing through a split in the hull.

"We're sinking," said Thyra.

"I can see that," Calder said.

1

"What are we going to do?"

Calder stood up and put a Visby lens to his eye.

"Borgarnes is near," he said.

"Will we make it?" said Thyra looking at the crack in the hull and the water spilling through it.

"It'll be close," said Calder.

He retook his seat and continued rowing. The storm eventually broke, and the port town came into view unassisted by the Visby lens. However, water was ankle-deep within the karvi longship, and Thyra and Calder's muscles were drained.

"Now I'm starting to wonder if we'll make it," said Calder, sweating much harder and more profusely than the much younger Thyra.

"Come on, Dad. You can do this," she said.

He laughed a little to himself, then pressed on. Together, they pushed themselves to their physical limits, but eventually, they reached the port just as the water in the ship hit their knees.

Calder dropped the oar in his lap and started panting.

"I'm getting too old for this," he whispered.

"You did great," said Thyra as she stood up in the knee-deep water and tied the longship to the pier.

"I'll get started patching the hull. You use that bucket to get the water out."

Thyra nodded and proceeded to do as instructed. The water went out slightly faster than it came in, and with Calder's work on the side of the ship, the water was only leaving. He then joined Thyra in evacuating the water, and the ship floated a few inches higher. Before long, the longship was mainly empty, and the two exited onto the pier.

"We'll need this ship professionally fixed, so we'll be in port longer than I'd hoped," said Calder.

"That's fine," Thyra said.

"Remember to stay close. People on the mainland aren't always the friendliest."

"I'm aware."

Thyra and Calder noticed the attention of passersby as they moved through the town towards the primary shopping district. They could hear whispering between folks but could not make out what they were saying—though they instinctively knew the gist of those private conversations. Thyra's white hair, pointed ears, and dark grey skin made her stand out. Thyra rolled her eyes, and Calder shook his head.

Borgarnes was the largest port town in all of Midgard. It was where roughly 75% of all shipping traffic originated and ended. It was a town that Calder's family was familiar with but one into which Thyra rarely ventured.

"Just ignore them," said Calder as Thyra watched those whispering folks pass them by in the street.

"Why are they like that?" she said.

"Ignorance," answered Calder.

They turned a corner that opened onto an expansive street filled with crowds of people and many different shops, restaurants, and mead halls.

"The place we're looking for isn't far," Calder said.

Various conversations unrelated to Calder and Thyra drowned out the whispering. The town was alive on this street. People moved this way and that. Horses were trotting along, guided by their owners. Carts carried all sorts of goods.

"I can get a sword here," said Thyra, observing a weaponsmith's shop to their right.

"You know how I feel about weapons," said Calder.

"When are those feelings going to change?" Thyra said.

"You don't need one."

"You used to carry a sword. I know that . . ."

"No, Thyra. No swords. An altercation does not always have to end in death," said Calder. "And that's final. Now let's find a shipbuilder to fix our karvi, and we can deliver our goods while they work."

Thyra let out a defeated sigh and followed Calder, navigating their way through the crowd of people until they came across a shop that fit their needs. The shop owner was busy working on a piece of wood.

"Excuse me," said Calder.

The woman looked up from her work.

"Can I help . . . oh no, not here," she said.

"Mam, we just need—"

"No. You two need to get out of here," the woman said, standing up and pointing at the door.

"Our ship has a crack in the hull. We need you—"

"If you two don't leave, I will yell for help," said the woman.

"Come on, Dad, let's go," insisted Thyra.

"All right, just one moment," said Calder.

"Help," shouted the woman.

Thyra was out the door as soon as the woman raised her voice. The woman stopped as soon as she was gone.

"You should be ashamed of yourself," whispered Calder.

"Me ashamed? Midgard settlements are for humans. Humans like you put us all in danger."

Calder shook his head and rejoined Thyra in the street.

"Are you ok?" he said.

"She's just a fool," said Thyra.

Thyra feigned a smile at the man who had raised her as his daughter.

"I don't know why people are this way," he said.

"Just go find a shipbuilder. I'll head back to our ship and wait for you there," said Thyra.

"Are you sure you're ok?" Calder said.

"I'm fine."

Calder opened his arms for an embrace.

"Dad, I don't need a hug. Seriously. I'll be ok," said Thyra, now putting some bass in her voice.

"Sorry. I'm gone," said Calder. "I will be back later with a shipbuilder, and we'll be on our way."

The two parted, and Thyra headed back for their slowly sinking longship. She endured more snickering and whispering as she retraced their steps from the pier.

"Humans," she said and took a seat on the longship.

Calder continued down the busy street of Borgarnes' business district in search of a shipbuilder that would fix their karvi so they could be on their way out of this port town. Not long after he had left Thyra, he came across another ship builder's storefront.

He entered to find a man putting away some of his tools.

"Can I help you?" said the man.

"I have a crack in the hull of my karvi longship," said Calder.

"Karvi . . . not doing much business, are you?" said the man.

"She's small, but she gets the job done."

The man finished situating his tools and looked at Calder.

"I saw you enter my competitor's shop just a moment ago. You were with that dark elf. Where is she?" said the man.

"If you're not going to give me your business because of her, then I don't want it," said Calder.

"Did I say I wasn't? How bad is the crack?"

"It isn't terrible, but we take on water quick enough that we'll be sunk before we are out of the bay," said Calder.

"Not easy being a dark elf in Midgard," said the man. "I know a little about that myself. My father, while not a dark elf, was not from this land. He crossed a vast distance to arrive in Midgard. People mistreated him greatly. Some mistreated me."

"Was your father from another realm?" said Calder.

"Another land," said the man. "My name is Bjarke."

"Calder."

"Let's go look at your ship," said Bjarke.

Thyra was standing at the stem of the longship, looking out at sea. Ships were coming and going as the sun was slowly setting. The storm they had passed through en route to Borgarnes dissipated hours ago. Her quiet moment of reflection was interrupted by the voices of Calder and Bjarke who were approaching the ship.

"I found someone who will fix our ship Thyra," said Calder.

She turned around to face him and Bjarke.

"Mam," said Bjarke.

She looked at the shipbuilder with a smidge of suspicion.

"You're ok doing work for a ship I own with my father?" she said.

"It's a fine ship, and I'd hate to see it sink to the bottom of the sea for foolish reasons," said Bjarke.

Thyra locked eyes with Bjarke, then looked at Calder, then back at Bjarke. She nodded and proceeded to grab the crates of mead she and Calder had been transporting.

"I guess we have work to do then," she said.

Calder smiled slightly and proceeded to assist Thyra with unloading their mead shipment.

"This won't take long to fix properly. You will need to give me a day. I have an inn attached to my shop. You can stay there if you like," said Bjarke.

"Is that ok with you, Thyra?" Calder said.

"Of course," she said.

"Very well. I will see you back at the shop then," said Bjarke.

Thyra and Calder left Bjarke to begin his work on their ship while they used carts to wheel the mead into town. There was a storehouse they supplied, and that was their destination.

The two walked in silence, avoiding the townspeople's snickering and whispering since the storehouse was at the edge of the town. Calder walked ahead of Thyra while Thyra stared aimlessly into the forest that hugged the town wall.

"Still thinking about that woman in town?" Calder asked.

"No," said Thyra. "Just thinking."

"What about? If you don't mind me asking?"

Thyra stopped pushing her cart.

"You knew my actual parents . . . did they ever feel . . . lost or alone?" asked Thyra.

Calder stopped and looked back at Thyra. A subtle breeze swept over the land.

"Your parents lived alongside my family for generations. Elves have the gift of longevity. You, too, will outlive me. You will outlive every human you ever know. While a long life can be a blessing . . . knowing that every relationship was ultimately very short did wear on your parents. They expressed this to me multiple times, yet they could not return to Svartalfheim to be amongst their people because they were still in hiding. When you were born, it was the first time I saw them truly elated. And yet they were terrified all the same. I cannot say that I know what you are going through, Thyra, but I can say that you are not alone in your thoughts about Midgard, humanity, and where you fit in in the world. We are not an easy species to be amongst. I know that. And you have never been around your own kind either. I want you to be happy, and I will do whatever I can to help you be happy. I hope you know that."

"I know that, Dad," said Thyra. "I just . . . it can be so lonely here."

"Your parents hoped humans would change. I hoped . . . hope they will too. But even I sometimes wonder if we will, especially after . . ."

"I know, Dad. I miss aunt Erika and her family also."

FEAR OF HUMANS

After delivering the mead to the storehouse, Thyra and Calder returned to Bjarke's shop and found the inn attached to the rear of the building. Bjarke was not there, so they let themselves in and took separate rooms on the second level.

Calder knocked on the door of Thyra's room.

"I saw a mead hall near the port earlier. Do you want to check it out?"

"No, I'm ok," said Thyra. "I might just go for a walk."

"I will go with you."

"It's ok. I want to . . . I want to go by myself."

"Thyra, it's . . . it can be dangerous."

"Dad."

"I know. I just worry. Please be careful. I know you're strong, but there are fools out there who will want to do you harm," said Calder.

"I'm aware."

"Ok," Calder whispered.

He did not leave.

"I'll be fine."

He nodded, then turned and headed for the stairs, but as he approached the end of the hallway, he heard his name called.

"Yes?" he said.

Thyra was standing in her doorway.

"Dad, I know you mean well, but I am an adult now," she said.

"I know you are. I have to remind myself of that sometimes."

They stood there looking at one another for a moment.

"Thyra, you don't . . . you don't have to be afraid of humans . . . we have a lot of growing to do. But you are special."

Then Calder turned and descended the stairs. Thyra remained in the doorway for a second longer before returning to the room.

"I'm heading to a mead hall for a bit," said Calder passing Bjarke, who had just returned.

"Your ship is coming along nicely. I should have it done tomorrow," said Bjarke.

"Thank you," Calder said.

Thyra waited by the window watching Calder walk off. She heard Bjarke put his tools away and ascend the stairs to his bedroom for the night. They exchanged kind words before he headed to bed, having spent the better of the day working on their longship.

Thyra heard the man snoring and got up. She decided to take the walk she had mentioned to Calder.

Meanwhile, Calder made it to the mead hall he had found and sat near a window that overlooked the port. He gestured for a pint, and a server brought him one seconds later.

The mead hall was bustling with patrons from all over Midgard who came to Borgarnes to do business. As he took a sip, his mind drifted to memories of his sister, her kids, and their family's sprawling mead business.

"This is almost as good as what Erika could do," he said to himself.

"Almost as good as who could do?" said the woman from the shipbuilder shop Thyra and Calder had attempted to patronize earlier in the day.

"Can I help you?" said Calder.

"You might be able to," said the woman.

She took a seat opposite him on the other side of the table. Then on either side of Calder sat two men, both much larger than he. Calder looked at them and put his mead down.

"I don't want any trouble," he said.

"Then why'd you bring it?" said the woman.

"What?" Calder asked.

"You know what I'm talking about," said the woman. "Don't play dumb. The dark elf. Where is she?"

Calder sighed.

"I have no idea what you're talking about," he said.

The man to his left grabbed Calder's arm tightly.

"Don't make this harder on yourself," he said, his voice deep and oddly unsettling.

"I'm telling you the truth," Calder lied. "I don't know what you're talking about."

"Let's get him out of here," said the woman.

With Calder's arm in his grasp, the man stood up and tugged on him to join him.

"Let's go," he said.

"I'm not going anywhere with you," said Calder raising his voice so the other folks in the mead hall would notice what was happening.

A few eyes shifted their gaze in his direction but most ignored him. He started to notice the faces of those who were whispering and snickering while he walked with Thyra.

"Cowards. All of you," shouted Calder.

A few more eyes looked his way, but then they averted their gaze.

"That's enough," said the woman. "Let's go."

Calder stood up, realizing his refusal to do so was futile. A few people watched as his aggressors escorted him out of the mead hall, but no one came to his aid. The three dragged Calder around the back of the mead hall, where one worker took out the garbage. He made eye contact with the group and returned inside the building, not wanting to be part of whatever was happening.

One of the large men punched Calder in the gut, the force of which made Calder double over and lose his breath. The woman grabbed Calder's chin and lifted his face to hers.

"Tell us where the dark elf is," she said.

Calder spit in her face. She jumped back, startled, and wiped her face clean.

.

"You're going to regret that."

The two men holding Calder proceeded to beat the man into submission. He fell to the ground in a fetal position as they continued to kick and hit him. After about a minute, they stopped, and Calder lay in the dirt, bloody and bruised.

The woman knelt to be just above eye level.

"This can go on all night or . . ."

"Or nothing," said Calder. "Do your worst."

"Fine then. You're almost as good," said the woman.

The two men lifted Calder to his feet. He could hardly stand, so they held him up by his shoulders as they dragged him behind the woman up the hill towards the edge of the forest surrounding Borgarnes.

Just beyond the tree line, the two men threw Calder to the ground. His body was so broken that it was hard for him to stand.

"You don't have to do this," he said.

"We'll give you one last chance to speak up then," said the woman.

"Never."

The woman nodded at one of the men, and he let Calder go. Calder watched him take the rope hanging from his belt and toss it over the highest and thickest branch he could reach. Calder struggled against the other man's grasp, but he hadn't been strong enough to free himself when he was not injured, but at this point, it was useless trying to fight back.

The man with the rope grabbed the dangling end and tied it into a noose. He then handed it to the woman.

"You would die for the dark elf?" said the woman.

"Without hesitation," answered Calder.

"All right."

The woman took the noose and placed it around Calder's neck. She pulled it tight and stepped backward. The man holding Calder let go of him, and the man holding the rope pulled with all his might. The rope went taught and lifted Calder into the air. His body flailed as he gasped for air. He yanked at the rope around his neck, but it was to no avail.

Thyra was passing through the street where she and Calder had looked for a shipbuilder. Her mind was all over the place. She thought about the people who snickered at her. She thought about the woman who would not let them hire her for shipbuilding. She thought about her parents, whom she had never really met. Then, she thought about Calder's offer to join him at the mead hall.

"I should have gone with him," she whispered to herself.

Thyra turned around and headed back to Bjarke's shop. She rapped on the open door. Bjarke was face down in his cot, asleep.

"Yes?" he grumbled.

"I'm sorry to wake you, but the mead hall my father went to . . . do you know where it is?" she said.

Bjarke let out a sigh and sat up.

"It isn't too often you see someone from another realm and a human traveling together, especially when that other-realmer calls the human their father. How'd you two come together?"

"My blood-parents passed a long time ago," said Thyra. "We just have always been together."

"Since you were a baby?" Bjarke said.

Thyra nodded.

"Midgard is a tough place for those who are different. I told your father this, but my father came from a land far away and looked nothing like the people of Midgard. He had a hard time, but he persevered and built a life for himself and his family. You seem like a strong young woman . . . stronger than the hate that pervades through Midgard."

"Midgard is my adopted home, and it's all I've ever known," said Thyra. "I still don't know why my blood parents left to come here."

"Whatever their reason, I'm sure it was not made lightly," said Bjarke. "Travel between the realms is significant, considering how rare Bifrost keys are."

"I'm aware," said Thyra.

"Right . . . sorry, you asked where the mead hall is. There is a large one near the port. That is most likely where your father went," said Bjarke.

"Thank you," Thyra said.

"Be careful, though. The fear and hate that people have can make them do unspeakable things, and the woman you encountered earlier is an especially nasty person."

Moments later, Thyra entered the mead hall where Bjarke had directed hers. A sudden hush washed over the entire hall as all eyes turned toward her. She scanned the room but did not see Calder. But one of the men working in the hall slowly raised his hand and pointed towards the backdoor. She walked past everyone en route to the door that the man had identified.

She exited the rear of the mead hall and saw signs of a struggle in the dirt.

"No," she whispered.

Thyra's eyes followed the tracks that led away from the struggle towards the forest surrounding Borgarnes.

"Be ok."

THREE

THREE SISTERS

Thyra scrambled to grab Calder's dangling body. She lifted him to create slack in the rope, took the noose from around his neck, and gently placed him on the ground. She put her ear to his chest.

"No, no, no, no, no . . ." she repeated. "Wake up. Wake up."

Thyra put her hand over his mouth. No air was escaping.

"Dad . . . Calder," she shouted.

"Savage creatures are they not?" said a mysterious voice from just behind Thyra and slightly over the top of her.

She turned around and saw three women, all with wings, dressed in armor, hovering in the air. Thyra stumbled backward, shocked to see Valkyries in the flesh. The one in front spoke again.

"Humans kill each other for such arbitrary reasons, but so do the gods, I guess, and humans more than any other species take after them the most," said the Valkyrie.

"Are you here to take him?" Thyra said.

"Maybe," said the lead Valkyrie.

"What does that mean?"

"It means maybe. We could be here to take him, or we could be here to give him a second chance . . . to give you a second chance with him."

Thyra stood up. She wiped the tears from her eyes.

"I've heard a lot of stories about Valkyries, but never any that referred to Valkyries offering second chances," said Thyra.

"And you've heard every story ever, have you? There is a first time for everything you know."

The three Valkyries descended to the ground so they were at eye level with Thyra. The leader extended her hand. Thyra looked at it.

"Hildr. The two behind me are my sisters, Svipul and Gunnr."

Reluctantly Thyra took Hildr's forearm into her hand. Hildr grasped Thyra's forearm, and the two women shook.

"It is a pleasure to meet you, Thyra."

"Will you save him?" she said, still extremely cautious and hesitant to truly engage.

"A Valkyrie's role in the nine realms is to oversee the life and death of great warriors, but most people focus only on the death aspect and ignore the life part. It's almost comical because one of the greatest healers in history was a Valkyrie," said Hildr.

"What are you suggesting?"

"We will save your father's life, but in exchange for something you have that we need," Hildr said.

"That I have?"

Hildr nodded.

"What could I have that Valkyries need?" she asked.

"A Bifrost key," Hildr answered.

"I don't have a Bifrost key. I would know, I'm sure."

"You're a dark elf in Midgard. You may have been born here, but your parents were not, and I caught wind of them years ago and have been keeping an eye ever since," said Hildr.

"You have been watching my family?"

"I just paid attention from time to time since they were fleeing Odin's war."

"What do you need a Bifrost for? You're Valkyries."

"We can travel to Valhalla and Helheim, but we are Midgardian Valkyries. Our station is here, and we need to go somewhere else," said Hildr. "Are you willing to make the deal? Your key for your father?"

Thyra hesitated and wiped the tears from her eyes. She looked down at Calder's body, then back at the Valkyries.

"If I knew where it was, yes," she said.

Hildr looked at Svipul and nodded. Svipul disappeared and moments later reappeared with the ghost of Calder. He was standing next to the Valkyrie. Around his neck were the markings of the rope that killed him.

"What is happening?" he said. "Thyra?"

"Dad!"

"Do we have a deal?" Hildr said.

"What is going on here?" Calder repeated.

"Father, do you know where the Bifrost key is?" Thyra asked.

He looked to his left and right at the Valkyries that surrounded him.

"What is happening? Are you bargaining with my life?"

"Do you know where it is?" Thyra said, raising her voice.

"Thyra, I don't think this is a good trade. I'm sorry but let me go."

Svipul and Gunnr looked at Hildr questioningly. A chilly wind swept over everyone.

"He knows where it is. Bring him back, and we'll get it for you," Thyra said.

Hildr turned to Svipul and gestured for her to revive Calder. Svipul knelt by Calder's body, and a golden glow emanated from her hands over his body.

"This is a mistake," said Calder's ghost as he faded.

At that moment, Thyra heard Calder's body gasp for air and saw the markings around his neck disappear. His eyes shot open, and he looked around.

"I'm alive," he whispered.

"I do have one ask of you three before we bring you the Bifrost. Tell me where the ones who did this are," said Thyra. "I know Valkyries have the ability to see the souls of the living and the dead."

"The souls of the dead are easy to spot, but the living are much more difficult. Fortunately for you, the three who did this are close," said Hildr.

Bodil, Dag, and Haldor sat around the roaring fire within the home of Bodil and Dag, drinking mead and laughing.

"Did you see the way his body flailed?" shouted Bodil, grasping her neck, mimicking Calder's final moments. "That'll teach him for bringing outsiders into Borgarnes.

"I thought you were going to absolutely lose it when he spit in your face," said Dag.

"I was about to," she said.

"What do you think will happen when the dark elf discovers he's gone?" said Haldor.

"Who cares?" Bodil said. "Maybe she'll take the hint and go home to be with her kind."

At that moment, the front door burst open and an enraged Thyra stood in the doorway.

"Or maybe she'll put down three animals," said Thyra.

"No," shouted Bodil standing up so quickly that her chair fell backward.

Haldor and Dag threw down their pints of mead. Haldor reached for his sword, but Thyra leaped between him and his weapon, grabbing his wrist and quickly breaking it. He shouted in pain and struggled to get free, but he could not fight against her grip.

"You thought you wanted me, but you just wanted to pick on someone you knew you could hurt. People hate dark elves because people fear dark elves," Thyra said coldly, still holding onto Haldor's limp wrist. "I'll give you a reason to fear us."

"Get out of here," shouted Bodil.

Bodil locked eyes with Thyra. She had denied fixing her ship, and now she was regretting that decision. She jumped at Thyra, but Thyra sidestepped her and swatted her to the ground with the back of her hand. Bodil crashed into Dag, taking him to the ground with her. Thyra let go of Haldor, and he scurried away from her.

"I came here wanting to kill you for what you did, but I can't let your madness infect me," said Thyra. "You three are hateful cowards who I am showing too much mercy."

With that, she turned for the door.

"Your kind doesn't belong here," shouted Bodil through tears and burning red cheeks. "Midgard will never have love for you."

"That may be so," said Thyra without turning around. "But I can't control your hate, only my own."

She stepped through the doorway and shut the three fools out of her life by closing the door. Outside were Hildr, Svipul, Gunnr, and Calder.

"Did you . . . ?" said Calder.

"I wanted to but . . . ," said Thyra.

"Now that we have held up our end of the bargain, it is time for you two to hold up yours. Take us to the Bifrost key so we can be on our way," said Hildr.

FOUR

FIMBULWINTER

Bjarke was an early riser. He poured himself some tea while the guests staying at his inn slept. He was careful not to wake them since he heard them come in late last night.

Bjarke sat his cup down in the kitchen and was out the door just as the sun was starting to crest over the Midgardian Sea. He strolled through the empty streets that were slowly beginning to come to life, past his competitor's shop, where he noticed the door was ajar and damaged, but there was no activity.

"That's strange," he said as he continued past her shop.

Bjarke did not stop to investigate further, and good thing he didn't, for he would have found an extremely pissed Bodil who may have directed her anger at him. Some people are slow to learn their lessons.

Bjarke arrived at the karvi longship of Thyra and Calder. The sun's rays washed over Borgarnes and its port, illuminating the ship and everything around it.

"There is definitely something charming about these smaller ships," Bjarke said to himself as he gazed upon the vessel. "So much attention is given to the big guys when these little ones do most of the work."

While Bjarke was getting started on the longship, Thyra was stirring in her cot. Her eyes were flickering as she exited sleep. She sat up and remembered the night before.

"Was it a dream?" she whispered.

But as she questioned the night's events, she felt a piece of paper slip through her hand onto the floor. She leaned over and grabbed it.

The note read, "Your key for your father. To not draw suspicion, we will return when your ship is finished. H. S. G."

"H. S. G," said Thyra. "Hildr, Svipul, and Gunnr. It wasn't a dream."

She placed the note on the bedstand by the cot and swung her feet onto the floor. Thyra got up and made her way to the adjacent room. Calder was still asleep.

"He's ok," she whispered.

She closed the door, noticed Bjarke was gone, and decided to visit him at the dock.

"This is a fine ship you two have here," he said.

"It's our last one," said Thyra.

"Oh?"

"The family used to have a fleet," she said. "That was back then, though."

"Something happened?" Bjarke said.

"I don't think much luck runs in this family," said Thyra looking out at the sea.

"Your ship will be finished today. I'll come get you when it is done," said Bjarke.

"Thank you. You've been a bright spot in a bleak town," Thyra said.

Hours later, Calder and Thyra paid Bjarke for their time at the inn and the repairs. The ship was as good as new. The damage that had stranded the two in Borgarnes was unnoticeable, and the vessel was seaworthy again.

Thyra boarded first, followed by Calder.

"Thank you," he said.

"Yes, thank you," said Thyra.

"The pleasure was all mine," Bjarke said.

With that, the two pushed off and were heading out to sea. It was a calm day. The sun was out but the few clouds dampened its beaming rays in the sky. A cool breeze washed over the ship, and the waters were still. Thyra sat near the bow of the ship on the starboard side.

"Do you want to talk about what happened?" Calder said, appearing behind her.

She turned around to face him, still startled by the memory of him lying dead.

"I thought I lost you," she said.

"I'm sure that was scary. I'm sorry," said Calder.

"I'm just glad you're ok now."

"The Valkyries who brought me back are wrong, though. They do not deserve your Bifrost key. Your parents left that for you to see your home one day."

Thyra got up from her seat. She started to pace.

"I didn't even know I had a key until a day ago," said Thyra. "Why didn't you tell me about it?"

"When your parents were killed, my sister and I hid the key. I always intended to make you aware of it. I realize now that I should have long ago."

"I see," she said, looking past Calder at sea.

"I understand if you are upset. I didn't mean to deceive or keep anything from you," said Calder.

"So, you know exactly where it is?" Thyra said without facing Calder.

"I do."

"Then you can show the Valkyries. You are my family, Calder. I want you to live."

Calder sighed and dropped his head.

"If that's what you want," he whispered.

Just then, three shadows passed overhead. Hildr, Svipul, and Gunnr descended from the sky, landing on the deck of the longship between Calder and Thyra.

"This is exciting. It has been a while since we have traveled by sea. You know if you head off in that direction." Hildr pointed east. "Rumor has it, that is where Thor faced Jörmungandr many years ago and where the World Serpent still swims."

"It's a good thing then we are not going in that direction," said Calder annoyed at the presence of the three Valkyries.

"I know you feel we are a burden, but rest assured, human, we will be out of your hair soon enough," Svipul said.

"What do you three Valkyries need a Bifrost key for anyway?" said Calder. "I heard you say you can only access Helheim and Valhalla, but what do you need to go to other realms for?"

"Am I missing something here?" said Hildr. "Did you forget the part about us saving your life in exchange for the key? I don't remember part of the bargain being you asking us what our intentions are, or am I mistaken?"

"How long until we get to your island?" said Gunnr.

"Just a day's journey," said Thyra.

"Then we can sit in silence until then," said Hildr.

"You can fly; why take a boat?" said Thyra.

"Because of the novelty," said Hildr. "We're in no rush at the moment. Let's enjoy the journey for now."

Calder and Thyra glanced at one another, then at the three Valkyries. They took up the oars on either side of the ship and proceeded to steer through the Midgardian Sea. The Valkyries stood about the ship but eventually took seats and watched Thyra and Calder work. The only sound was the sea crashing against the sides of the karvi longship and the calm breeze that washed over everything.

Hours passed like this. The calm was uneasy, and the trip was absent of any overt drama, but there was a tension that existed. It was a tension felt more by Thyra and Calder than by the three Valkyries, and for a good reason.

"We are approaching our home," said Calder as the island came into view on the horizon.

Hildr, Svipul, and Gunnr each glanced at one another in anticipation.

"Once we make land, I will go retrieve Thyra's Bifrost key for you," said Calder. "Unless, of course, Thyra—"

"Don't go there," said Hildr. "The deal has been made. And I think it is wise that you, Calder, remember that deal."

"I haven't forgotten," he said.

"It's ok, Dad," said Thyra. "Show them where it is."

Thyra and Calder steered the longship into the dock that led up to the farm they called home. Thyra tied the ship in place, and everyone departed. Since their time at sea, a few clouds had formed that blocked out the sun, casting the island in a shadow.

"You can all wait here." Calder pointed at the cottage. "I'll grab the key."

"They can wait. I'll come with you," said Hildr.

"Sure," said Calder.

"We'll keep an eye on the elf," said Svipul.

Gunnr nodded in agreement.

Calder and Hildr left the group, heading toward the forest edge surrounding the small farm.

"How'd you come to raise a dark elf?" said Hildr.

"What is this?" said Calder. "Why do you care?"

"I can't make conversation? We are not adversaries. I saved your life. I would say we are allies."

"What is happening here? All this is strange. I appreciate you bringing me back, but the key you are after is for Thyra."

"I think she would rather have her father."

"She will outlive me anyway and needs to be able to see her home one day."

Hildr stopped. She placed a hand on Calder's shoulder, and he stopped too.

"There is a change coming to Midgard, and it isn't a good change. And it is going to affect all species, humans up through Valkyries. We might be inconveniencing you and your daughter but believe me when I say we are not your enemy. Your problem is much bigger."

"What are you talking about?" Calder asked.

"The Great Winter."

"Are you sure?" said Calder.

"I can sense it. And now I've told you more than I need to. Let's get this key so we can be on our way."

"Skítur," whispered Calder.

Hildr started walking again, but Calder remained still. Hildr snapped her fingers to get his attention. He looked up and continued.

Thyra, Svipul, and Gunnr waited in silence at the cottage. Thyra observed the two Valkyries. She had never seen Valkyries in person, only heard of them in stories like most people. Their wings were not as pronounced as she thought they would be, but their armor was stunning and visually striking.

"Where will you go once you get the key?" said Thyra, breaking the silence.

"That isn't your concern," said Svipul.

"I can't be interested?" said Thyra. "We have time to talk."

"How did you end up in the care of a single human?"

"My parents died shortly after I was born."

"Have you ever wondered about your home realm?" said Gunnr.

"Of course."

"And you really did not know you had a Bifrost?" Gunnr said.

"Yes," Thyra said.

"Most people would know, especially if they were from another realm. It makes me wonder if you do care about your home realm."

"I think about where I come from . . . where my parents came from, all the time."

"What about why your parents came to Midgard?" said Gunnr.

"I know what happened in Svartalfheim during the war between the Aesir and Vanir. How dark elves were slaughtered. I know that's what drove my parents to Midgard."

"A slaughter is putting things lightly," whispered Svipul.

"If you really want to know why we need the Bifrost key, I'll tell you," Gunnr said.

"She doesn't need to know," said Svipul.

"It isn't going to change anything if she knows or not. Besides, Hildr has surely told her father. Our sister has a big mouth." Gunnr said. "Fimbulwinter is almost upon us. Hildr, Svipul, and I have no desire to be around for Ragnarök that follows."

"And a Bifrost key will let you avoid the end times?" Thyra asked skeptically.

"Yes," said Gunnr.

Thyra let out a deep sigh.

"If Ragnarök really is near, shouldn't we all be preparing?" said Thyra.

"Prepare for what? Something that is destined? Something that was foretold thousands of years ago? If we were going to prepare—we had time. There is no preparing for this. We just have to do what we can to survive it," said Gunnr.

"Gunnr, that's enough," said Svipul. "Let's just wait until Hildr and the human return, and we can be on our way."

"Sorry," she whispered and turned away from Thyra.

Moments later, the farm door opened, and Hildr and Calder walked through it. In Hildr's hand was a small device.

"We got it," she said.

Calder looked at Thyra and hung his head.

Hildr held up the key.

"It needs to be charged, but there is a cave where the power of the World Tree is highly concentrated on this island," she said.

"I'm sorry, Thyra," Calder said.

"We thank you for what you've done for us today," said Hildr. "Svipul, Gunnr, let's go. We've intruded on these two for long enough."

And with Hildr saying that, the three Valkyries headed for the door. Hildr and Svipul exited first, but Gunnr stopped in the doorway.

"Remember what I said. Fimbulwinter."

And with that, she too disappeared out the door.

FIVE

THE VISITOR IN WHITE

Thyra and Calder stood in the empty room of the farmhouse, having just been left by the three Valkyries.

"I . . ."

"Don't apologize. I wanted them to have the key. You are more important than that," said Thyra.

"When my sister and her husband and kids died, I would have given anything to get them back. But just because you would give anything does not mean that you should."

"Dad. . . . No. I couldn't trade your life. Seeing you dead on the ground was the worst experience of my life. I am fully aware that one day you'll be gone. I know that. I am a dark elf, and we live for thousands of years. But the day you do pass cannot be today."

"Thyra . . . ," said Calder holding up a small gem.

"What is that?"

"It's the part of the Bifrost key that stores the energy of the World Tree that makes it work."

"So, they won't be able to charge it?"

"Giving them the key got them off our back for a little bit so we can think freely."

"Why would you do that?" shouted Thyra. "When they find out you've deceived them—"

"We'll be ready."

"Ready? Ready for what? Dad, they're Valkyries, and there are three of them. Valkyries are the fiercest warriors in the nine realms. What are we going to do? You were killed by a group of humans—no offense, but you aren't exactly a fighter."

"Violence is not the solution all the time.

"Have you forgotten where we live? Dad, this is Midgard."

"No realm is without violence, Thyra. And if we are to get better, we'll need to think beyond it. Envision what we want the realms to be like and act accordingly."

"Dad, I want you to be ok."

"Our lives are finite, Thyra, but you will have the longevity to see the realms of the World Tree improve, but only if you believe they can. These Valkyries . . . they're up to no good. You and I both know that. And their leader mentioned that the end times are near. They are planning to evade it somehow, but they have hope, and so do I."

"Dad, you are an idealist."

"I made a promise to your parents that one day, you would get to see your home, and I won't break that promise."

Twenty-five Years Ago

Ase sat on the dock near the farmhouse, looking out at sea, holding baby Thyra. Hagen approached from behind her, bringing two cups of tea.

"Beautiful day," he said.

Ase looked back at her husband.

"It is," she said.

"Almost two centuries looking at this view, and it has not gotten old yet," said Hagen.

He sat one of the cups down on the table next to Ase.

"We really made a life here," said Ase.

"We did."

"Want to hold her?"

Hagen nodded and put his cup of tea on the same table.

"She is lovely," he said.

"She is the future," said Ase.

Hagen lifted baby Thyra into the air and observed his daughter with the backdrop of the Midgardian Sea. He felt his eyes starting to swell.

"I am so happy," he said. "Happier than I've been in so long."

"Me too," said Ase watching her husband hold their daughter.

There was a calm between the two dark elves and their baby. It was a quiet that was interrupted by Erika.

"Who is that?" said Erika as she approached from the farmhouse.

"What are you talking about?" asked Ase, turning around to face her.

Erika pointed out to the sea, redirecting Ase's gaze. A ship was approaching.

"Your brother?" Ase said.

"Calder is here," said Erika. "And I don't recognize that craft."

Ase and Hagen glanced at each other.

"Vikings?" said Hagen.

"Ship is too small for a worthwhile raid," said Erika. "I doubt it's Vikings."

"Take Thyra inside," said Ase to Hagen.

"What are you going to do?" he said.

"I'm going to see who this is," she answered.

"Erika, tell your parents an unknown ship is approaching the island. They'll probably want to get ready."

"Get ready for what?"

"Just go tell them."

Erika nodded and ran off.

"Hagen, watch our daughter no matter what," said Ase.

"I will. But what is going on? Who is that?" he said.

"I don't know, but my gut tells me it's not good," she said.

"Then you take our daughter, and I'll greet this person."

"Hagen, go. If something happens, only you can teach our daughter about her heritage. Remember. She was your mother."

"You're starting to worry me," Hagen said.

Ase looked out at the sea. The boat was much closer now.

"Go," she said.

Hagen nodded and took Thyra up to the farmhouse. Ase walked to the edge of the dock and waited. A storm cloud pushed in front of the sun casting the island and the approaching ship in a vast shadow as if mother nature were outwardly expressing the feeling of dread building deep inside Ase.

As the ship neared, she could make out a single person standing at the helm as the winds that brought the storm clouds pushed the ship. The person she could see was a man dressed in white, an outfit that Ase was familiar with from long, long ago.

"It can't be," she whispered.

Oili and Manning ran to Ase's side, having been warned of the approaching ship by their daughter.

"Who is it?" said Manning.

"I don't know how he found us. . . ." whispered Ase. "It's been so long . . . I thought . . ."

"Who is it?" repeated Manning.

"Make sure everyone is well hidden, but first, Manning, bring me my sword."

"What?" he asked.

Ase said, "Get my sword. Then hide with your family."

"Come on, honey," said Oili. "Let us do as she says. We have to let Calder know, and Erika too."

"Sword. Hide. Got it."

Moments later, Manning reappeared with Ase's weapon as instructed, then disappeared to join the others. Ase stepped up to the very edge of the dock with the sheathed sword by her side and the hilt in her hand.

The storm clouds darkened, and the face of the man she hoped she would never see again came into clear view. Her grip on the sword was so tight that her knuckles turned white. Small droplets started to fall as the longship pulled up to the dock.

"Long time," said the man.

Ase did not reply.

Inside the farmhouse, everyone shuffled into the basement below and fanned out into the expansive mead storehouse.

"What is happening?" asked Calder to no person in particular.

Hagen answered, "Someone was approaching by boat that spooked my wife. She wants us to hide while she deals with it."

"Who is it?"

"I'm starting to think I know, and if it's who I think it is, she is going to need help," said Hagen while looking at his daughter Thyra.

"We can watch Thyra," said Erika.

"You all know these rooms connect to tunnels your ancestor Erlend started for storing mead. They span the entire island. Follow the path to the other side and leave for the mainland. There will be a place for you to stop at our cottage en route. I need you to grab the Bifrost key we keep above the fireplace. That is for Thyra when she is ready and when Svartalfheim is ready, explained Hagen.

"We can do it," said Calder.

"Good. Let's move because Ase doesn't have much time."

The raindrops that started as small pellets turned into massive droplets in just a few minutes, and in that same amount of time, the unwelcomed guest to Erlend Island was forcing Ase to fight for her life. Ase was more desperate than she had been in almost two hundred years. Her left shoulder had a gaping wound with blood flowing the length of her arm. Her legs had bruising all over, and her chest felt fragile. Ase's breathing was heavy. She was losing, and the end was nigh.

"You always were far more skilled than the others. Perhaps that gave you a false sense of hope," said the man, who, unlike Ase, was completely unharmed, though he was just a little winded. "But a skilled warrior pales in comparison to a god."

"You are not a god," said Ase between deep breaths.

"Not yet."

Ase went into a rage with renewed vigor. She unleashed a spectacular assault, which would have spelled certain doom for any normal person on the receiving end. She was like a berserker. But the unwelcomed guest dipped, dodged, and deflected as necessary and ultimately swatted her away, sending Ase flying through the air and tumbling through the mud.

The man walked up to her as she attempted to get up. She looked up, and he put a knife to her throat.

"I know you won't tell me where your daughter and husband are, but this island is small. And even if they are not here now, they'll come back eventually."

"I will die before you get them," said Ase.

"You will die. That I can assure you," said the man.

He went to cut her neck, but a blast of energy impacted against his back, knocking him away from Ase. He tumbled through the dirt before catching his footing. Ase saw standing behind him, Hagen, his hands glowing.

"What are you doing?" shouted Ase.

"I'm saving you," he said.

Ase watched Hagen unleash a wave of energy with a reddish hue onto the visitor before running over to help her to her feet.

"I told you to take Thyra and go," she said.

"I couldn't let you face him alone," said Hagen.

"Thyra is more important than either of us."

"She will be ok."

From the farmhouse, Erika and Calder could see the pier where Hagen and Ase were engaged in battle with an unknown visitor in white.

"Who is that?' said Erika.

"He looks like a light elf," said Calder. "The white robe and his ears are like theirs."

"Are they going to make it? That doesn't look like a battle. That looks one-sided," said Erika.

"We're going to need to revise Hagen's plan," said Calder.

"What are you proposing?" Oili asked.

Calder ran inside the cottage, grabbed the Bifrost off the mantle, where Hagen said it would be, and returned to his family.

"We hide," he said. "There is no way if they lose that this guy won't find us at sea. But the caves span the entire island, as Hagen said. I think we can wait him out there."

"And we could also be lost forever," said Manning.

"Calder is right, Dad," said Erika. "Best case scenario, Ase and Hagen win. But if they don't and we attempt to flee, we'll be picked off easily at sea."

"What about using the Bifrost?" said Oili.

"No idea how," said Erika.

"And rumor is humans can't," added Calder.

"So, our choices are either to hide in a potentially damning maze of tunnels or escape to sea where we'll likely be picked off?" said Oili.

Erika and Calder both nodded.

"Skítur," whispered Oili.

Ase helped Hagen to his feet after the most recent exchange with the visitor. He was also in the same shape she had been when he arrived—bloodied, bruised, and exhausted.

"Peacetime has made you both weak. I do remember more fight out of you before."

"Is this it for us?" whispered Ase.

"Our daughter will live on," said Hagen.

"She'll be alone in this world."

"For now, but she has a way home."

"I love you," said Ase.

"I love you too."

The explosion from the battlefield by the water shook the ground underneath the feet of Erika and Calder as they helped their parents and Thyra back into the cavern. Then Erika went ahead of Calder. As she slipped underground, he took one last look down by the sea, and as the smoke cleared, he saw Hagen and Ase fall.

Tears formed at the corner of his eyes.

"Goodbye, you two," he whispered.

Present

"To this day, I don't know who showed up on the island, but your parents gave their lives to save ours . . . to save yours. And they wanted you to have that Bifrost key so that you could one day return to Svartalfheim. You cannot give it to those Valkyries," Calder said.

Thyra let out a long sigh as she ran her hand through her hair.

"All this time, and I never knew how my parents died," she whispered.

"The man who came for them scoured the island for a week and eventually left. I haven't seen or heard from him since. We buried your parents when it was safe to return above ground and hid the Bifrost key. Eventually, life returned to partial normalcy. My sister formed her own family and took on the mead business, but you know how that story ends."

"You feel this strongly about the key?" said Thyra.

Calder nodded.

"I do."

"All right. Let's get the key back."

SIX

SEEING RUNES

Hildr, Svipul, and Gunnr took flight after they received the Bifrost key from Calder and Thyra. A strong wind had picked up since their arrival. The clouds covering the island had darkened, blacking out the sun.

"Thor? Odin?" asked Gunnr.

"We have not caught their attention yet," said Hildr. "But maybe it is better we start to hurry up."

"You're the one who opted to take a boat here."

The Valkyrie sisters flapped their powerful wings, propelling them through the skies. Their destination was a cave on the island far north of the cottage.

Hildr held the key out in front of her as she flew. She looked it over and smiled.

"Almost free," she whispered.

Meanwhile, Calder and Thyra saddled up two horses from the stable. Calder grabbed a sheathed sword and handed it to Thyra.

"But I thought you said no swords. . . ." she said.

"I might be an idealist, but I'm not a fool. I hope we don't need them."

"They are not going to just accept an exchange, Dad, and you know we can't beat them in a fight," said Thyra.

"That's ok," said Calder. "They are heading to a place where the energy of the World Tree flows through Midgard. It is the reason your parents chose this island long, long ago. We will get the Bifrost key, reconnect the gem, charge it, and Bifrost out of there. They'll have no way of knowing where we went."

"You know how to use it?"

"You will have to do it. Bifrost keys only work for those with a strong connection to the World Tree. Elves, dark and light, the Vanir and Aesir, and Valkyries. But I can ride along, though."

"Steal the key, charge the key, use the key," said Thyra. "Did I get that right?"

"Hopefully, it's simple as that."

"We'll see, Dad."

Hildr led while Svipul and Gunnr followed. They had been flying for only a few minutes when Hildr pointed at the ground.

"Down there," she said.

The trio descended from the air, landing at the mouth of a small cave.

"Can you feel it?" said Hildr.

"Yes. The World Tree's power is strong there," said Svipul.

They cautiously walked up to the edge of the cave and stopped right at the entrance. Each looked at one another before crossing the threshold.

At the same time, Thyra and Calder were charging through the dense forest of Erlend Island on horseback. Calder led and Thyra followed. The wind whipped over them in a frenzy, and branches snapped under the foot of the mighty steeds. Thyra's heartbeat pounded like crazy in anticipation of their confrontation with the Valkyries. Calder, too was very nervous though he was reluctant to let on to that fact. The forest broke, and the two found themselves on a partially cleared pathway.

"Not much further now," said Calder.

"They'll beat us there."

"That's ok."

The cave was alive in a way that no other cave was. It surged with an invisible current that could be felt but not seen save for the sparks of electricity that occasionally arced amongst the stalactites. The three Valkyries walked with a cautious respect for the power that flowed within this cave and the access point to the World Tree, which connected the nine realms.

As they went deeper and deeper, a dim light started to show. It started small like a far-off star in the night sky, but as the trio approached, it grew. It was the access point to the World Tree, and it glowed beautifully white. It was bright, but strangely they could look directly at it without having to avert their gaze.

"Amazing," said Hildr as they walked up to the stream of energy rising from a deep well in the cave, dissipating as it impacted against the ceiling.

"How does it work?" said Gunnr.

Hildr held up the Bifrost key.

She inspected it and said, "I think I just hold it in the river of energy for a few seconds."

Thyra and Calder slowed their horses from a gallop to a walk as the cave's entrance came into view. Calder inspected the skies.

"They must be inside already."

"Are you ready?" said Thyra.

Calder pulled on the reins, and his horse stopped. Thyra followed suit. He looked back at her.

"What is it?" she asked.

"On the off chance this does not go in our favor, you need to promise me something."

"Dad, don't even think like that."

"Thyra, I am serious."

"And so am I."

"Listen to me. There is a reason aside from the fact that I promised your parents you would one day see your home of Svartalfheim that I don't want these Valkyries to have your key, and I think you should know it."

"I'm listening," said Thyra.

"Your parents were fleeing a war-torn realm thanks to Odin, so one of the first things they did upon arriving in Midgard was using a seeing rune to make sure things would be ok here. They looked as far into the future as they could, and the only thing they said they saw that seemed dangerous were three winged strangers. I think Hildr, Svipul, and Gunnr are those three strangers. Whatever they want with your key is for something nefarious."

"But they didn't see the man who killed them?" said Thyra.

"Seeing runes highlight moments of note to the person using them. The impact of these Valkyries must have weighed heavier for your parents than their own death. Also, the further into the future seeing runes project, the fuzzier the prediction becomes. But despite all that, your parents warned me of the Valkyries, and I'm telling you—they cannot get their hands on your Bifrost key."

"What could they be up to?" said Thyra.

"Valkyries are powerful creatures. They're motivated by Ragnarök, which could push them to the extreme. If these three do not get what they want, they may go on the offensive. If that happens, I do not know how to defeat them or if they even can be defeated, but there is one man who does. His name is Mimir. He is an ancient being from before my time who used to consult the Allfather. Your parents told me all about him also. His presence in Midgard is what drew them to our realm."

"I thought this access point to the World Tree is what attracted them?" said Thyra.

"That is what brought them to our island, but Mimir brought them to Midgard in the first place. His consultation is without rival. He told them about this island."

"Where is Mimir?"

"A place called Mímisbrunnr. It is on the mainland. Your parents told me he is no fan of Odin or any of his kin, which Valkyries very much are. He should be able to help you if . . ."

"If you are killed," said Thyra.

Calder nodded.

"It won't come to that," she said.

Thyra pushed her heels into her horse, and the beast started trotting again. Calder watched for a few seconds, then followed suit.

"But it may," whispered Calder. "And I am sorry."

In the cave, Hildr, Svipul, and Gunnr were growing frustrated. The Bifrost key would not hold any of the energy passing over and through the device. Unbeknownst to them, it was missing the storage gem, but also unbeknownst to them, the storage gem was being brought their way.

"The human did something," said Hildr. "I know it."

"He sabotaged the key somehow," said Svipul.

"He couldn't have. I was with him the whole time."

"Somehow, he tricked you," said Gunnr.

"We must force him to fix this," said Hildr.

Hildr put the key by her side.

"Let's go," she said.

"No need," said Calder, seen in the light of the World Tree access point. "I'm here."

"Where's the dark elf?" said Hildr.

"Came alone," he said.

"We can just scan for her," said Hildr.

"Not in here; you can't," said Calder. "I met a Valkyrie long ago during my travels as a mead dealer. She was nice. She told me a lot about your kind. The energy you seek when you do your duties as a Valkyrie is currently all around us. I'm no expert on your kind, but I imagine your senses would be overloaded down here."

"He's right," said Svipul. "I can't see him or anything other than what's coming from the root."

"What did you do to the Bifrost key?"

"That key is not for you," said Calder. "It belongs to Thyra."

Hildr spied the sword attached to Calder's hip.

"Came to do battle, did you?" she said. "What do you hope to achieve, human? You can't defeat us."

"Don't play with him," said Gunnr. "Make him tell us what he did to the key."

Hildr put a hand up to quiet Gunnr.

"I have this under control," she said.

Hildr walked closer to Calder.

"You're lucky. In the past, my sister would simply torture you into telling us what you did, but she has relaxed, and I am more reasonable than that. I think it's easier to revoke the intervention we made on your behalf and deliver you straight to Helheim, where you'll spend eternity in the shadow of the Goddess Hel as one of the damned, forced to forgo an eternity in Valhalla."

"Helheim?" said Calder.

"The realm of the dishonored dead," said Hildr.

"So be it then."

"You would voluntarily go to Helheim?" said Hildr.

"No. I will give you the piece of the key you're missing and show you how it works."

"I knew you would see it our way eventually," said Hildr.

From the shadows, Thyra watched Calder move towards the Valkyries. She heard the conversation and waited for her moment to strike.

SEVEN

POWER DEEP WITHIN

The energy that flowed from the well in the center of the cave was immense and flooded the cave in a warm glow. But unlike the sun that shined so bright or a fire that burned too hot, one could stare directly at this energy without averting their gaze and let it wash over them without being hurt. It took hold of you like an embrace from a loved one.

Years ago, Calder last stepped inside this cave and looked upon the energy. He had almost forgotten the feeling it provided.

He approached the well from which the energy rose as Hildr, Svipul, and Gunnr stood around him.

"For as long as my family has lived on the island, this connection to the World Tree has been here," he said. "And I know it dates back to long before us."

"It is beautiful," said Hildr.

"I know that an ash tree stands called Yggdrasil, a high tree, soaked with shining loam; from there comes the dews which fall in the valley, ever green, it stands over the well of fate," whispered Calder.

"Show us how it works," Hildr said, placing a hand on Calder's shoulder.

He reached into his pocket, an act that, for Thyra, was a signal.

Calder took out the gem.

Hildr, Svipul, and Gunnr all looked at one another, acknowledging the piece missing from the Bifrost key.

"How did you take that without me noticing?" said Hildr.

"It was never with the key, to begin with. I hid it elsewhere just to be safe," he answered.

He walked over to the well. The power of the World Tree was rushing all around him, arcs of electricity bouncing around the cave's ceiling. The gem started to glow as it got closer to the river of energy.

"That stores the power for the key?" asked Hildr.

Calder nodded and proceeded to plunge the gem into the light stream. The small jewel tickled the palm of his hand as it charged, and a rainbow glowed around his fist. He gripped it tighter as he felt the immense energy of the World Tree consumed by the tiny orb.

"Is it working?" said Svipul.

"It appears to be," answered Hildr.

"It's working," said Calder as a rainbow glow proceeded halfway up his arm.

"We'll be Odin's pawns no more," whispered Gunnr.

As Calder held the gem in the energy of the World Tree, he felt the orb getting warmer and saw the rainbow glowing brighter but then both stopped. The warmth and the glow reached a peak. He took this to mean the small stone had charged completely.

"I need the Bifrost," he said.

"No. You give me the jewel," said Hildr. "We have had enough of your tricks."

"I'm a human. I cannot use a Bifrost key. You know that. But this jewel has enough power stored in it to kill all of us if it isn't loaded into the key properly. Just let me do it, so you're not escorting me and yourselves to Helheim."

Hildr looked at Gunnr and Svipul.

"Just do it," said Gunnr. "He's right. Humans can't use the key. And if he tries anything, I'll kill him."

"I agree with Gunnr," said Svipul. "I'm ready to get this over with."

"Fine," Hildr said.

She handed the Bifrost key to Calder. He took it into the opposite hand of the one which held the gem. He flipped a small hatch on the bottom of the key and positioned the gem at the entrance. Hildr, Svipul, and Gunnr gathered around him as he did so.

The gem slipped inside the Bifrost key, and Calder closed the hatch. Immediately the teleportation device started to glow from its core. Hildr moved to snatch the device away from Calder. However, as she did so, she was beaten by Thyra, who had taken the device only half a second before.

Calder felt Thyra put a hand on his shoulder, and as the device activated, an ultra-bright rainbow shined down over them. Hildr quickly grabbed Thyra, and the three disappeared from within the cave, leaving behind Svipul and Gunnr.

The rainbow touched down outside Borgarnes in the forest surrounding the port town. The explosion of energy leveled some brush and sent birds scattering in all different directions.

Immediately Thyra attached the Bifrost to her waist and pushed Calder away from Hildr, who was still holding onto her arm.

"Dad, run," she shouted as she wrapped her hand around Hildr's arm.

"I knew you could not be trusted," shouted Hildr attempting to pull away from Thyra. "Let me go."

Calder watched as Hildr sprouted her massive wings and flapped them twice to aid in pulling away from Thyra, but Thyra was strong, and her grip was powerful. The two women were lifted into the air together.

"Let go of her," shouted Calder as Thyra went higher and higher up.

"Dad, just run. I can handle her."

"You can try," said Hildr turning her attention away from Calder and onto Thyra.

Hildr stopped rising and, with a mighty push from her wings, shot towards an exposed branch on the nearest tree. Thyra's back was to the branch, and she would be impaled. She grabbed Hildr's other arm and swung her weight underneath the Valkyrie, pulling Hildr slightly downward so that her face was where Thyra's body had been. Now in a position where she would be the one impaled, Hildr stopped the charge midflight and redirected for the ground.

Hildr dragged Thyra along the ground, weaving around trees and through thickets until Thyra lost her grip on one of Hildr's arms. She then quickly spun, so the sudden jerking motion freed her other arm. Thyra went flying and crashed through bushes, ultimately stopping at the base of a massive tree.

Thyra let out a deep sigh and wiped the sweat from her brow.

"Enough," shouted Hildr, descending with her wings outstretched, spanning almost ten feet.

Thyra put a hand on her knee and pulled herself to her feet. She was scratched up, and her pelt tattered. Thyra reached for the sword attached to her waist but instantly noticed its absence. She spied it lying on the ground behind the Valkyrie. It must have fallen off when she went crashing to the ground.

"You can't keep this up," said Hildr touching down. "A dark elf you may be, but you are no Valkyrie. I'm by myself right now, and look how you're struggling. Once my sisters get here, you will stand no chance. And that's if you last that long. And I will let you in on a secret: Gunnr is stronger and more ruthless than me."

"I'm no pushover, and I will do what I must," said Thyra.

"But you don't have to do this. Give me the Bifrost.

Thyra looked at the key attached to her waist.

"Thyra don't," shouted Calder.

"Stay out of this human."

"Dad, I just . . ."

"Remember what I said . . . it's not just about your home."

"I have had it with you two," whispered Hildr.

Hildr charged Thyra. She grabbed the dark elf by the neck and slammed her into the tree behind her. The bark splintered, and leaves fell. Thyra kneed the Valkyrie in the abdomen, but it was to no avail. Hildr merely shrugged off the strike and placed a second hand around Thyra's neck.

"Is this what you want? To die here for a key that you only just learned about? There are so few of you left. Think about what you're doing."

"No one is going to die here today," shouted Thyra.

"You are a fool, child. If not your father, then you will die." Hildr said through gritted teeth.

Thyra's eyes and fists glowed red. A surge of energy exploded from within her, and Hildr went flying.

"That was . . . different," Hildr whispered, and she righted herself.

Calder ran up to Thyra after she blew Hildr away.

"Are you ok?" he said almost frantically.

"I'm fine."

"Let's go while we have a chance," he said.

Thyra lifted the key and reached for Calder's hand, but as she prepared to trigger the device, she felt Calder grab her firmly.

"Move," shouted Calder, turning Thyra around so that he was between her and the blade flying through the air.

The sword speared him the whole way through, immediately bringing him to his knees. Calder's blood painted Thyra's face. For a second, she was in shock and could not process what had just happened. One moment, they were about to escape; the next, she looked at her father on his knees, blood seeping from a gaping hole in his chest. The Bifrost key slipped from her hand and landed in the dirt. The gem that powered it fell from within the key and landed at Thyra's feet.

"That's one way to undo our intervention," whispered Hildr.

"Dad," Thyra shouted. "Dad."

Calder looked down at the sword protruding from his abdomen.

"Thyra," he said. "You have . . . to get . . . out of here . . . take . . . the key."

"Dad, I can't leave."

"There's no . . . time . . . go . . . now . . . or we'll . . . both be killed."

Thyra approached her father and knelt in front of him.

"You can't leave me here," she whispered.

"You're not . . . alone, Thyra. I'll always . . . be by your side."

The color from his skin quickly faded, and Calder's head dropped. His body slumped forward, held up only by the sword stuck into the ground. Thyra closed his eyes and carefully situated him on his side. She looked up at Hildr, who was hovering in the air. Thyra's eyes were glowing red, and the ground around her started to tremble.

A bolt of lightning struck down behind Thyra. Hildr looked around and saw storm clouds forming overhead.

"Thor?" she whispered.

"Look what you've done," shouted Thyra. "You won't get away with this."

The clouds darkened, and more and more flashes of lightning touched down all around Thyra. The ground shook violently.

"This power," said Hildr. "It's not the power of a dark elf. What are you?"

But just as Hildr was starting to worry, Svipul and Gunnr appeared by her side.

"Took you two long enough," she said.

"It took a little bit to lock onto your energy," said Svipul. "That cave was potent. What happened?"

"I killed the human," said Hildr. "It was an accident."

"And she started glowing?" Svipul said. "Dark elves don't have this kind of power . . . do they? Is she something else?"

Thyra's right hand had a bright, crimson aura surrounding it. She raised it into the air and then slammed it to the ground. An explosion of dirt skyrocketed around her. When it dissipated, she and Calder's body were gone.

"I can't detect her," said Hildr.

"Doesn't matter. She left the key," said Gunnr. "And her father."

Standing where Thyra had been was the ghost of Calder. The three Valkyries descended to the ground and surrounded him. Gunnr picked up the key and shook her head.

"What?" said Hildr.

Gunnr showed her the bottom of the key. The gem was not inside.

"Back to square one," said Gunnr.

"This would have been a lot easier for you if you had just cooperated with us. But instead, you made it so the last thing you said to your daughter was a lie. You will not be by her side," said Hildr.

"You don't scare me," said Calder.

"I may not. But trust me when I say . . . the Goddess of Hel will. Svipul, deliver him to Helheim, then meet us back at the Hall. We have to regroup."

"Come on, human," said Svipul putting a hand on Calder's shoulder.

From behind a few massive trees and bushes, Thyra watched the three Valkyries disappear. The red glow that had emanated from her had faded, and her eyes returned to the dark brown they usually were. Tears streamed down her cheeks, her fists clenched so tight that skin broke in her palms.

"Damn you," she whispered.

Thyra picked up Calder's body when she felt comfortable that the Valkyries were not returning. She moved from her hiding spot and looked around. Her explosion had cleared the area of any plant life and left a crater behind. Only broken tree limbs, dirt, and rock remained.

"How did that happen?" she whispered.

She turned her free palm upward, contemplating what power existed within her. But it was then she heard horses and men shouting. People from the port town of Borgarnes were coming her way. Unwilling and incapable of explaining herself, Thyra, carrying Calder, took off in the opposite direction, heading deeper into the forest.

She did not stop until she could no longer hear anyone and the shadows from the mountainous trees were so dense it was as if nightfall had come early. It was then she laid Calder down on the forest floor. He looked oddly peaceful for having perished so violently.

"Dad," she whispered. "Why? Why did you do that?"

Thyra looked at the glowing gem from the Bifrost key.

"For this?" Thyra said.

She turned and started clearing foliage. It took her an hour to dig a grave deep enough for Calder. She then proceeded to place him in it and cover him with dirt. She collected rocks of varying sizes and created the outline of a ship around his grave.

Upon completion, she stood by the side of the grave and said, "Lo, there do I see my father. Lo, there do I see my mother and my sisters and my brothers. Lo, there do I see the line of my people back to the beginning. Lo, there do they call to me; they bid me take my place among them in the halls of Valhalla, where thine enemies have been vanquished, where the brave shall live forever. Nor shall we mourn but rejoice for those that have died the glorious death."

EIGHT

NOT THAT SLEIPNIR

Thyra's body was bruised, scratched, and beaten. She was tired and miserable. Never was she in such a dark place or felt so alone. Walking through the dense forest without direction, she remembered her life with Calder. He had always been there. She knew one day he would not be, considering the vast difference in the average life spans of their respective species, but she still saw that as a far-off occurrence. She had not prepared for it to happen so soon.

The place where she buried Calder was now far away. Thyra was walking aimlessly and had been for hours since putting him to rest in the ground and saying a prayer. The sun set long ago, and the moon cast rays through the treetops. Small critters were scurrying about the forest floor, and an owl was hooting somewhere unseen.

Thyra stopped and looked up.

"Why did you take him?" she whispered.

She looked at the moon through an opening in the trees. Its spherical shape reminded her of the gem in her pocket. Thyra took the gem into her hand. Its glow had faded a little from the use of the Bifrost key, but it was still warm. She inspected it.

"Three Valkyries were willing to stray from their normal duties and kill to obtain a Bifrost. What could drive them to do that?"

Thyra continued to look at the gem. The energy it had absorbed swirled within it like a cloud of stars.

"It is beautiful," she whispered.

Thyra slipped the gem back into her pocket.

"Enough feeling bad for yourself," she said. "Those three will be looking for this, and I can't let dad's death be in vain."

The hooting of the owl was louder. Either it had flown closer to her, or she had walked near it. Either way, the noise the creature made drew her focus.

"Mimir," she whispered. "I need a map."

Thyra turned around. Borgarnes was the nearest town she knew; fortunately, she knew someone there.

Bjarke was peacefully sleeping when he heard a knock at his door. He stirred in his cot, blinking his eyes awake. Someone knocked again. He propped himself up on his elbows.

"Who could be here at this hour?" he whispered.

He swung his feet over the edge of his cot and rested them against the cold floor. Someone knocked a third time.

"Hold on; I'm coming."

He got out of bed and made his way downstairs to his shop.

"Who is it?" he said through the door. "What do you want?"

"It's Thyra. I need your help."

The door shot open. Bjarke grabbed Thyra by the arm, pulled her inside, and slammed the door behind her.

"Did anyone see you?" he said, sounding extremely worried.

"No. It's so early in the morning. No one is out."

"The people of this town are in a frenzy," Bjarke said. "They're blaming you for the explosion in the woods and that you're on some rampage."

"I did cause the explosion," said Thyra.

Bjarke did not respond right away. He just looked at Thyra curiously. Then he said, "How?"

"I don't know," said Thyra. "We were attacked, and it just happened."

"Where is your father?"

Thyra shook her head.

Bjarke looked at the ground.

"I'm sorry."

"I need a map and a horse. Can you help me with that?"

"I have a map," said Bjarke. "No horse, unfortunately."

He headed for the kitchen and rummaged through the cabinets for a few moments until he found his map. He brought it to Thyra and laid it on a table in front of her.

"Where are you heading?" he said.

"Mímisbrunnr."

"I don't think I've ever heard of it," he said, pouring over the map closely. "And I don't see it on here."

"That's a map of all of Midgard?"

"It is. The most up to date too."

"How can you find something that's unmarked?" Thyra asked rhetorically.

"You find someone who has been there," said Bjarke. "This town here, Hlíðarendi, is home to a highly respected warrior named Gunnar Hámundarson. He is one of the most well-traveled people in all of Midgard. If anyone has heard of this place you seek, it will be him."

"This is a multi-day journey on foot," whispered Thyra to herself.

"Bodil is the woman who claims you attacked her, and she has a horse. It is her prized possession, and it is still early."

"Thank you," said Thyra.

Bjarke drew a circle around Hlíðarendi with chalk, rolled up the map, and handed it to Thyra.

"Travel safely, and I hope you find what you're looking for."

Thyra extended her hand.

Bjarke grabbed her forearm, and she did the same to him. They shook once, and she left, map in hand.

As the sun rose, Bodil felt its warmth wash over her. She had hardly slept since such an eventful night and wanted to stay asleep, but she had to feed her pet—the only good thing in her life. She nudged Dag to move so she could get out of bed. He grumbled but moved so she could slide past him.

Bodil walked downstairs and grabbed a candle to light the torch in the stable. Once she hit the first floor of her home, she immediately sensed a change or an absence. She wiped the sleep from her eyes and lit a torch by the door.

She dropped the candle and shouted, "Sleipnir."

Thyra felt the wind washing over her face as the mighty steed raced down the Midgardian road in the rising sun.

"I can't believe she named you Sleipnir," said Thyra.

Sleipnir whinnied.

"You think it's funny, too, don't you?"

The horse whinnied again.

Thyra pulled on the reins and slowed Sleipnir to a walk. She grabbed the map and scanned it.

"Making good time," she whispered. "We should be there by this evening."

NINE

THE RUNE WRITER

Hildr, Svipul, and Gunnr landed outside the doors of a great hall. Hildr pushed open the doors, and the three entered the arena with torches burning along both sides. A giant mural of the World Tree decorated the wall furthest from the entrance.

"None of what just happened went according to plan," said Gunnr. "What do we do now?"

Hildr took a seat on the bench under the mural. She turned and looked up at the image of Yggdrasil.

"Without that key," she whispered. "All of this is out of our reach, and so is our survival."

"We know that," said Gunnr. "So, what now?"

At that moment, a door to the left of the mural opened, and a tall woman with broad shoulders and white hair walked into the room. She wore a black cloak and a satchel.

"I heard you return," said the woman.

She scanned the three Valkyries and saw the defeat on their faces.

"You don't have the Bifrost?"

Hildr held up the key.

"We don't have the gem that holds its power," she said.

"How did that happen?"

"The dark elf has some latent abilities we did not account for, but no matter . . . we have you. Gunnhild, we need your talents now," said Hildr.

"But your physiology won't—"

"Gunnhild, remember why we saved you," said Hildr. "We've already taken one soul to Helheim today. Don't be the second."

"I haven't forgotten. But you know why you need the key."

"We know. Svipul, you go first. Then you Gunnr. Come fetch me when you've finished," said Hildr.

With that, she left the three in the hall and exited the building. Hildr looked up at the blue sky dotted with clouds.

"It's all so peaceful now. . . ."

The hall doors opened, and Gunnr was standing by Hildr.

"We are still going to have to fight," Gunnr said.

"Yes, but at least we'll have a chance," said Hildr. "That's all we need . . . that is all any of us need."

"What about the dark elves?"

"The nine realms are tough, and some are less fortunate than others."

"Are you sure what we are doing is right?"

Hildr stopped gazing at the sky and turned to Gunnr.

"You're asking me that?"

"I am capable of questioning my actions. Are you?"

"We've already started down this path, Gunnr. It's too late to turn back now."

"Is it?"

"Valkyries who stray rarely live long and fulfilling lives," Hildr said. "The only one is Eir, but she lives in seclusion."

"And we can't do the same?"

Hildr shook her head slowly.

"In the end, we'll all be called to battle. Eir too. The goal is to survive that battle. Do not forget, we all committed to this together."

"And I'm prepared to do what I must, but I just want to be sure that what I must do is necessary and not just the path of least resistance."

"If there was another way . . . Odin and his son Thor are Tyrants . . . never forget that."

"I haven't . . . but are we becoming them?" asked Gunnr.

"They do what they want. We are doing what we must. There is a difference."

"Not to the oppressed," said Gunnr.

Gunnhild cleared a table inside the temple and rolled an animal hide over it. She then gestured for Svipul to lie down face up. Svipul did so and closed her eyes. Gunnhild opened her satchel and set various tools on the bench next to her. She opened a small jar. Svipul peeked over at her.

"Like usual, I just need some of your blood to mix with the ash," said Gunnhild.

Svipul nodded and gave Gunnhild her arm. She made a small incision and let the blood flow into the container, mixing the contents of the jar thoroughly.

"Ready?" Gunnhild said.

Svipul nodded, and Gunnhild produced a long needle.

Outside, Gunnr and Hildr stood in silence.

"There will be a day when we don't have to live like this . . . but that day is still a long time from now," said Hildr.

Gunnr put a hand on Hildr's shoulder. A gentle breeze washed over them, and Hildr looked back at her.

"We are with you," said Gunnr.

Hildr nodded subtly.

Hours Later

The hall doors parted, and out walked Svipul, covered head to toe in runic markings. Hildr and Gunnr were gathered around a fire. They both turned to see their sister.

"Always impressive," said Hildr.

"Gunnhild does not disappoint," said Gunnr.

Gunnhild appeared alongside Svipul.

"Gunnr, you're up next. I must work quickly; these tattoos won't last long, and as you know, they are time-consuming."

Gunnr looked at Hildr.

"We're almost there," said Hildr.

T E N

GUNNAR

As nightfall befell Midgard, Thyra brought Sleipnir to a slow trot as she approached the wall that protected Hlíðarendi. More than aware of humanity's impression of dark elves, Thyra steered the horse off the main road and into the woods that lined it.

"Easy boy," she said and pulled on the reins so Sleipnir would stop.

Thyra looked up at the wall and contemplated how she would get over it. There was a man at the gate. She could see him in his watchtower. Thyra hopped off the horse.

The horse whinnied as Thyra gently touched the animal's face.

"Any ideas?" she said playfully.

The horse whinnied again.

"Didn't think so."

She walked up to the edge of the wall and touched it. It was sturdy but not indestructible. With whatever it was that she found in herself to fend off the Valkyries, she could probably tear a hole in the wall, but two things were stopping her. First, she wished to remain stealthy and blasting her way in was the opposite of stealth. But the second was the bigger issue; she had no clue how to channel that power.

Thyra turned her palms towards her and tried to manifest the same red glow she had channeled before, but nothing happened.

She looked up at the guard again. He did not seem to be paying much attention to what was happening beyond the gate. It appeared he was drinking tea and writing.

"Hmph."

The man at the gate was reading about the runic works of Ragna Unn. No one other than his mother knew he was studying to become a rune writer. The pot of tea he'd brought with him for his guard shift made the reading much more pleasant, but rune writing was a complicated art.

"How does anyone get this stuff?" he said to himself.

Just then, a knock at the gate caught his attention. He sat the text down and placed his cup of tea next to it.

"What now?" he said.

He peered over the edge of his watch tower and saw a single horse rapping its hooves against the door.

"What's going on?" he whispered.

He stood up to get a better vantage.

"Where's your rider?" he said.

The horse neighed and beat its hooves against the door a second time.

"Ok, I'm coming," said the man.

He grabbed the ladder and descended the watch tower.

"What is going on?" he whispered as he pulled the chain lever to open the gate slightly.

The horse backed away as the door parted, and the man walked out.

"Where's your rider, girl?" he said, approaching the horse.

The creature neighed and raised its two front legs high into the sky.

"Easy now," said the man. "Easy."

While the single guard was distracted, Thyra slipped behind him and through the open gate.

"Well done, Sleipnir," she whispered.

"Who are you?" said another guard looking Thyra in the face.

Thyra dropped her hood.

"A dark elf," whispered the man.

His eyes grew wide. Acting fast, Thyra tackled him to the ground and put him in a choke hold. She held him tight until he fell unconscious. Then she quickly pulled him into the shadows.

"Igor," said the man outside the gate. "Come help me with this horse."

Thyra looked at the gate.

"Oh no," she said.

"Igor, what are you doing? Come help me."

Thyra heard the man fighting with Sleipnir but knew he would eventually deem the struggle not worth it and return to see his fellow guard, Igor, was missing. She made the rational decision and snuck back through the gate.

"Igor, finally," said the man, hearing but not seeing Thyra's approach. "Help me get this thing under control. I don't know where it came from."

Thyra did not immediately answer and instead started to reach for the guard to knock him unconscious the same way she had done his partner. However, as she reached for him, she felt a hand on her shoulder. She stopped and looked back. A man with broad shoulders and white hair was standing before her. He shook his head and gestured for her to follow him. She hesitated, then did as instructed.

"Igor," said the guard, turning around as Thyra and the mysterious man who had summoned her disappeared around the corner. "What is going on here?"

Thyra and the man stopped at a cottage.

He fiddled with the door, but before he could open it, Thyra said, "Who are you?"

"The one you came to speak with. Gunnar Hámundarson."

Thyra took a seat near the door as Gunnar threw a log onto a low-burning fire in the stove of his cottage. He grabbed a tea kettle and situated it above the fire. He handed a cup to Thyra.

"Thank you," she said.

"You're wondering how I found you when it was you who was looking for me. Am I correct?"

Thyra nodded.

"Would you be surprised if I said my reasoning was prophetic?"

"No."

"Months ago, I was told to wait for a visitor by the gate. That someone unlike any who had ever stepped foot in Hlíðarendi would arrive on this night. When I saw you were a dark elf, I knew it had to be you."

"Who told you to wait for me?"

"Mimir."

"Can he see the future?"

"Not to my knowledge, but I'm sure he would tell you how he knew you would come here."

The tea kettle started to whistle. Gunnar removed it from the flame and poured the hot water into Thyra's cup.

"Why did you wait, and why did you stop me from knocking out the other guard?"

"As opposed to ignoring Mimir?"

Thyra nodded.

"Can I say duty? And the guard you knocked out was not working. He was just passing through. If you would have incapacitated the one who was on duty, his replacement who was coming in an hour would have noticed and put the town on high alert."

"I see."

"I listened to Mimir and found you because Mimir told me you have a gift that would be useful in battle. Something, unlike the nine realms, has seen in ages."

"You want me to help you fight someone? I can't control this gift."

"The second great war is coming for us all. I have seen the signs of the end approaching. Someone like you with a special gift will be an asset to the people of Midgard."

"And what if I don't want to be an asset to the people of Midgard?"

"Let me revise my statement . . . you will be an asset to the beings of the nine realms."

"How do you know this?"

"It is not hard to tell. You just have to look for the signs of creatures acting strangely."

"Like three Valkyries seeking a Bifrost key?"

"Exactly like that. Is that something you have seen?"

Thyra nodded, then watched Gunnar take a sip of his tee.

"Is there something on your mind?" said Gunnar.

"Humans aren't too keen on dark elves. I understand you see my gift as valuable, but why are you so hospitable?"

"I know what happened to your people . . . at least the broad strokes. I know there are not many of you left. I know that because there are not many of you, stories can be made up, and there isn't any way for you to refute them."

"Nor should we have to," said Thyra.

"Humans live short lives, and most of us are scared. We cluster into towns because we are scared, and fear gets applied to all things we don't know or care to understand. Aside from a long life and being slightly stronger, dark elves, light elves, and humans are physically the same. Long ago, our species even used to intermarry."

"How do you know that?"

"Because I am part dark elf."

"You're a human and a dark elf?"

"Just a tiny bit at this point. One of my ancestors was a dark elf. But things changed after the Great War. I've seen some of the most heinous acts against others, perpetrated by humans more than any other creature. Even if the claims against your kind were true, they'd be no worse than what I've seen my own people do, and I know not all humans are bad, so not all dark elves can be bad."

"Humans killed my father . . . they killed him because he was with me."

"I'm sorry."

There was silence between the two. The fire cracked.

"You came to Hlíðarendi for a reason. You're looking for Mimir? How can I help?"

Thyra picked up the cup of tea and took a sip.

"You know where he is? I'm assuming since he told you about me," she said.

"Yes. I can help you find him. I can also show you where to find better gear for your journey. Your horse was a fine creature. The guard will have taken her to Hrimthur, one of Midgard's finest horse breeders. I am sure you will want to get her back. I will also take you to meet with Bo, arguably humanity's greatest swordsmith."

"Thank you."

"You can rest if you like. I doubt the guard you put to sleep is waking up any time soon . . . or we can go now. I'm sure neither Bo nor Hrimthur have headed to bed yet."

"I would rather not wait," said Thyra.

"Very well. Follow me."

Thyra hung back with her hood up as Gunnar rapped on Bo's door.

"Who is knocking on my door at this hour?" said Bo from the other side of the door.

"Bo, don't kid yourself; I know you aren't anywhere near your bedtime. It's Gunnar. Open up."

The door shot open. Standing in the doorway was a stocky fellow with a black beard.

"Come on in," he said.

Gunnar turned around and waved for Thyra to follow.

"Who is that?"

"A friend. Let us talk inside."

"Make yourselves at home," said Bo gesturing for the two to enter.

Thyra kept her hood up as she passed him. Bo looked up and down the alley his home was situated on before closing the door. There was no one. It was eerily tranquil.

"Gunnar, to what do I owe the pleasure?" said Bo.

"Thyra, you can remove the hood. You're amongst friends," said Gunnar.

Slowly she revealed her face.

Bo gulped.

"A dark elf," he whispered.

"Thyra is a friend. I vouched for you that you would help her. Was I mistaken?"

"Look, I'm not trying to be rude, but . . ."

"You are being rude," said Gunnar.

"I have not seen . . . one of her kind up close before."

"Apologize."

"I'm sorry."

"This man is supposed to help me?" said Thyra to Gunnar.

"Bo is a skilled weaponsmith even if sometimes he is a fool," said Gunnar looking at Bo.

"I'm sorry," said Bo.

"Three Valkyries have barged into my life and killed the only person I ever loved, and they are planning more supposedly. I need to find Mimir to figure out what is going on and, if necessary, how to stop them," said Thyra, choosing to ignore Bo's gaffe.

"Valkyries?" said Bo.

He looked at Gunnar.

"I didn't know." He turned to Thyra. "The Valkyries looking for a Bifrost that you mentioned earlier are after your Bifrost?"

"Yes."

"There is a Valkyrie named Eir who lives here in Hlíðarendi, though at the moment she is away with her husband in Fensalir. She is kind. What you are describing does not sound like the actions of a Valkyrie," said Bo.

"And you know all Valkyries?" said Thyra. "I wish what I was telling you was a lie, but there are three of them. Their names are Hildr, Gunnr, and Svipul. They showed up wanting a Bifrost key I did not know I had, and when my father would not give it to them, their leader Hildr killed him. She was trying to kill me, but he stepped between myself and the blade."

Bo and Gunnar looked at one another curiously.

"If a group of Valkyries has turned . . . what does that mean?" said Bo.

"Valkyries are the most dutiful creatures in the nine realms. Only Eir ever traded in her responsibilities, and that was because she had a child with a human," said Gunnar. "Perhaps we Fimbulwinter is sooner than I thought."

"The end times?" said Bo.

"Thyra, this mission you're on . . . its implications may be far-reaching. I'm going to come with you. We need to learn everything we can from Mimir."

"I can't ask you to do that, Gunnar."

"I have to."

"Gunnar, she is right. Remember Gissur the White."

"Gissur can wait."

"You know that isn't true."

Gunnar clinched his fist.

"Then Bo, make sure she has the best sword you've crafted."

"Of course."

Thyra watched Bo move across the room to a table at the rear. He pushed aside the table, revealing a door in the floor, and pulled it open. A staircase descended beneath the home.

"Gunnar, hand me a torch," said Bo.

He did as instructed, and Bo moved underground. He reemerged a few moments later.

"Ok, come take a look," he said.

Thyra followed Bo and led Gunnar underground into a basement well-lit with flickering torches and well-stocked with Bo's finest work.

"Only the best for a friend of Gunnar."

"Haven't been down here in a while," said Gunnar.

Thyra scanned the various weapons, swords, axes, and gauntlets before settling on a glowing sword hanging at the far wall.

"How much for this one?" she said.

"You have quite the eye. That is Gambanteinn. Before its blade, giants will bend," said Bo.

He pulled the weapon from the wall and handed it to Thyra. It was perfectly balanced and other-worldly sharp.

"That was the first blade I forged after I finished my tutelage under the dwarf Eitri, the same dwarf who forged Thor's mighty hammer, Mjolnir."

"You studied under a dwarf?" said Thyra spinning the blade in her hand.

"I did," he said. "Years ago, when I lived in Lejre."

"Bo is one of the few humans who has had that privilege," said Gunnar.

"Take the sword. I want you to have it. It's a gift," he said.

"I have gold," said Thyra.

"And yet it is still a gift."

Thyra sheathed the blade and hitched it to her belt.

"Thank you," she said.

"Let's get your horse so you can be on your way," said Gunnr.

As Thyra and Gunnar approached the stable that housed Sleipnir, Thyra asked, "Why would he give me such a weapon?" I did not earn this."

"Bo is incredibly loyal to Eir, the Valkyrie he spoke of earlier. To know that there are three of her kind terrorizing an innocent is surely upending his world. He gave you that sword as a means to do what is right."

Like, Bo, Hrimthur was also still up at this late hour. He had just finished situating Sleipnir in his stable when Gunnar and Thyra knocked at his door.

"What now?" Bo said.

He opened his door and saw Gunnar and Thyra standing before him. Hrimthur observed each of them and then gestured for them to enter.

The two entered, and Hrimthur shut the door behind them.

"Gunnar, you have many allies, but I never thought one would be a dark elf," he said. "Welcome."

"Hrimthur, the horse you just received is hers," said Gunnar.

"And here I thought I just got lucky. That's a beautiful creature."

"I should be on my way," said Thyra.

"My stable is around back," said Hrimthur.

He led Thyra and Gunnar to where he kept Sleipnir. The saddle was hanging by the stall door.

"I'll get her fixed up for you," he said.

As Hrimthur got to work, Gunnar rummaged through his satchel and took out a map. He unrolled it and handed it to Thyra. He pointed to a place north of their current location.

"Mimir is here at Mímisbrunnr. Only those who have been there before can tell you how to get there."

"Isn't that how all locations work?" said Thyra.

"Give it a try. I just showed you where the location is. Go tell Hrimthur."

Not believing Gunnar, Thyra summoned Hrimthur to her side.

"What is it?" he said.

"Mímisbrunnr . . . have you been?"

"No."

"Well, it's . . ."

She scanned the map.

"What sort of magic is this?"

"See?" said Gunnar.

"That's impossible. You just showed me."

"Only those who have visited Mimir can tell you where he is," said Gunnar.

"Are we done with this?" said Hrimthur growing impatient. "I haven't finished preparing your horse, and I would really like to get to bed sometime this week."

"Yes. Sorry," said Thyra.

"Mimir is a sagacious fellow and should be able to help you on your journey, wherever it takes you," said Gunnar.

Thyra rolled up the map and stuck it in her pelt.

"Thank you," she said.

"Don't thank me yet. This quest you are on. It won't be easy. I don't know why three Valkyries would do what they've done, but I can tell you that whatever drove them to do it was no small matter. Valkyries are powerful creatures. I know you said you're different but be careful."

"I will," said Thyra.

"And think about what I said. You can be an ally to all the realms."

"I hear you."

"Good luck."

Hrimthur led Sleipnir out of her stall and handed the reins to Thyra. She mounted the mighty creature with a new weapon and a known destination.

ELEVEN

SAVED FROM THE WORLD SERPENT

Six Months Ago

The last thing Gunnhild could recall was falling overboard into the Midgardian Sea, yet she was not wet. She patted her pelts. Nothing. Gunnhild looked around. She was on land.

"What happened?" she whispered. "What is happening?"

"Welcome back."

Gunnhild looked up in the direction of the voice and saw a Valkyrie hovering above her, rays of light shining from behind her, obscuring her face.

"I'm dead?"

The Valkyrie descended and touched the ground.

"My name is Hildr," said Hildr. "And no, you are not dead. I saved you. Your skills as a rune writer would have gone to waste at the bottom of the sea."

"Eric," said Gunnhild.

"Your husband is fine. He survived, but most of your crew did not."

"What now? Will you return me to him?"

Hildr shook her head.

"No," she said. "Not yet. You have some work to do for me and my sisters."

"So, what is this? I'm your slave?"

"Let's say you have a debt to me," said Hildr. "A debt that you will pay. We need your help."

"I appreciate you saving my life, but I have a husband and a life to return to. What if I refuse to do your bidding?"

"I'll feed you to the World Serpent alongside the rest of your men."

Gunnhild looked at the ground. Only moments ago, she was with her beloved and their crew traveling the Midgardian Sea when the World Serpent capsized their longship. Now she was with this Valkyrie whose intentions she did not know.

"What do you need from me?" said Gunnhild. "What can a human do for a Valkyrie?"

"Don't sell yourself so short. You're not just any human. You are one of Midgard's most skilled rune writers. I'm lucky to have had the opportunity to save you from death," said Hildr with a sinister smile. "Take my hand. I will introduce you to my sisters."

Hildr extended her hand, and reluctantly Gunnhild took it. The two took flight and shortly after arrived at an old hall. Torches were burning along the walls. The flight was unsettling for Gunnhild. She stumbled upon arriving in the hall.

"You will get used to traveling like that," said Hildr.

"Not sure I will," said Gunnhild.

"Sisters. I found her."

From behind Gunnhild appeared Svipul and Gunnr. She turned to face the other two approaching Valkyries. They were equal in stature to the one who had rescued her from drowning.

"So, our sister saved you, and now, you're going to save us," said Gunnr. "She's old for a human."

"More time spent practicing my craft," said Gunnhild.

Gunnr cracked half a smile.

"What am I doing here?" Gunnhild said.

Hildr nodded to Svipul. Svipul grabbed a bag full of supplies from the room she and Gunnr had come from and laid the bag at Gunnhild's feet.

"What's this?"

"Open it," said Hildr.

Gunnhild knelt by the bag and pried it apart. She reached in and pulled out containers of ash and a tattooing pen.

"I know your specialty," said Hildr. "The work you did for your husband, you can do for us."

"If I do this, will you return me to him?" said Gunnhild.

Hildr looked at her sisters. They nodded.

"Yes," said Hildr. "I will."

"Then tell me what you need your tattoos to do."

MY NAME IS HELGA

Thyra steered Sleipnir off the road into the trees that lined it. They trotted along for a few minutes until she felt sufficiently hidden from any passersby in the night. When she felt comfortable, Thyra dismounted and tied Sleipnir to a large tree, then proceeded to lay a few large stones in a circle. She gathered wood and not before long had a fire going.

"What am I doing?" she whispered, looking into the dancing flames. "What can I do?"

Her mind drifted to a memory of an exchange between her and Calder when she was young.

"You can do anything you set your mind to, Thyra. You are strong, and one day all the realms will know what I know," said Calder.

"What do you know?"

"That you are special. And that no one can tell you otherwise."

The memory faded, and Thyra wiped a tear from the corner of her left eye. The wood in the fire cracked and popped.

"I'm sorry, Dad, that I wasn't stronger."

She looked up at the night sky. It was clear, dark, and filled with stars. Before she knew it, she was asleep.

When Thyra awoke, the fire embers were glowing and covered in ash. She immediately sensed another presence and shifted her gaze to the right. Sitting near the fire, warming her hands, was a young girl.

Thyra sat up immediately.

"Who are you?" she said, quite startled.

The girl pulled her hands away from the fire and looked at Thyra.

"My name is Helga. You can let go of your sword. I mean you no harm."

Thyra looked down at her hand. She was reflexively grasping the hilt of her weapon. Slowly, cautiously, she let go.

"You summoned me here," said Helga.

"I summoned you here?"

Helga nodded.

"You did," she said.

"What are you?"

"I am a flygja . . . I am your flygja," said Helga.

"A flygja . . . a protector spirit?"

"Let us say companion spirit for now. I have yet to participate in a battle. Who knows how I would fair?"

"Why me?"

"A good question. I don't know. I just showed up here a moment ago."

"You don't know where you came from or why you are here?"

"Do you know anything about yourself before you were born?"

"I know who my parents were," said Thyra.

"And I know who you are. But that does not answer my question."

"You're not messing with me, are you?"

"Look around you. We are in the middle of nowhere. Where would I have come from?"

"And you do look like a child. I guess a child wouldn't just be this far from any town."

"Probably not."

"Why do you look like a child? I thought a flygja looked like their creator or sometimes an animal?"

"I am fairly certain we can take many different forms."

There was a pause between them.

"It's cold these days," said Helga.

"It is almost winter."

Helga looked at Thyra.

"What are we doing? What's the plan?"

"*I* am on my way to visit Mimir so that I can figure out what is going on with these Valkyries that ruined my life and inquire about how to defeat them if that is necessary."

"What happened?" said Helga.

"They killed my father."

"And this ruined your life?"

Thyra looked at Helga curiously and answered, "Yes."

"Is it over?"

"Excuse me?"

"Is your life over?" said Helga.

"What kind of flygja are you?"

"What kinds are there?"

Thyra turned to face the embers.

"The stories I have heard describe you as helpers. You protect and do things to assist those who manifest you."

"Am I not doing that?"

"You seem just to be bothering me."

Thyra stood up and kicked dirt onto the hot coals. She situated the few supplies she had laid out to sleep and placed them in the saddle on Sleipnir. The sun had yet to rise, but it was less than an hour away.

"Are we leaving?" asked Helga, standing up as well.

"We? Helga, I do not know how or where you came from, but it's just me on this journey. I already told one person I'm doing this alone. I'm not—"

"I'm not a person," said Helga. "And you can't just get rid of me. I'm here because of you."

"I only have one horse," said Thyra grasping at anything that might deter this girl.

"Not a problem."

Helga levitated off the ground.

"The Valkyries are dangerous."

"Thyra, whether you like it or not, my fate is linked to yours. I'm coming with you on this journey."

Thyra pinched the bridge of her nose and sighed.

"Ok," she said.

"Think of me as the sister you always wanted."

"I never wanted a sister."

"That might be what you told yourself . . . but I'm inside your head, and it is a mess there. So much conflict."

"You can read my mind?"

"Not quite. It's more like we share a mind. Or more accurately—shared a mind."

"So, you could just be part of my imagination?"

Helga stopped levitating and picked up a rock.

"I am as real as you are. I am not made up. I am a living being that was born of you. I can be hurt. I can be killed. Though I share your mind now, you and I will drift apart since we are not one. But I am here to support you on your journey."

Thyra stared intensely at Helga, the young girl standing before her. Her eyes were old, and her hair was long and flowing. She wore a cream-colored dress with no shoes.

"I have many questions but not enough time to go through them. So . . . if you are here to help, let's be on our way."

THIRTEEN

BLOOD. ASH. TATTOOS

Three Months Ago

Gunnr opened the room to where Hildr was resting with anger spread across her face.

"What?" Hildr said.

Gunnr held out her forearms.

"Again," she said.

Hildr sat up and inspected her sister's arms.

"They're fading . . . again. This rune writer you found . . . maybe she is not up to the task."

"This is impossible," said Hildr, concern starting to take her. "She used the highest quality ash in all of Midgard, and what can be better than our blood?"

Gunnr shook her head.

"I don't know, but she needs to figure this out because this is the fifth time, and nothing is changing."

"Where is she?" said Hildr.

"By the river."

Gunnr followed Hildr out of the hall, down the hillside where Gunnhild was standing, looking out at the Midgardian landscape.

"They're fading again?" said Gunnhild without turning to face the two Valkyrie sisters.

"Why isn't this working?" said Hildr. "There is no purer ash than what we provided for the most recent runic drawings."

Gunnhild looked down before turning around.

"I've been thinking about this all morning. I do not believe it is the ash that is the problem."

"And what is?" said Hildr.

There was a silence between the three women, and then Gunnhild spoke up.

"Valkyries are special creatures . . . very different than practically all the other species of the nine realms—"

"We know this," said Gunnr.

"Yes, of course, you do. Your bodies heal at an extremely fast pace. Faster than anything I have ever seen. By mixing your blood with the ash, your body simply heals and repels the blood and ash mixture used to draw the runic tattoos. Your bodies are cycling through the old blood because it doesn't see it as part of you anymore and because your bodies heal so fast, it just gets rid of it . . . ash included."

"And what is your solution? Because without these tattoos—"

Hildr held up her hand, gesturing for her sister to stop talking.

"You need to use something your body won't reject so quickly. I say Valkyries are special creatures because it is as if you are all creatures at once. Godlike and yet not gods, mortal and yet not mortal. Your physiology is representative of what you are, a bridge between worlds; because of this, I think your body would be receptive to different blood types. Your body rejects your own because once it's been removed from your body and mixed with the ash, you no longer recognize it, which starts the healing process. The blood that was removed is effectively dead and must be flushed away."

"What are you suggesting?" said Hildr losing patience.

"I think we need to use a blood that your body won't recognize as dead as soon as we mix it with ash and tattoo it back onto your body, and because Valkyries are receptive to the blood of all creatures in the nine realms, using another specie's blood won't poison you."

"But wouldn't we run into the same problem?"

"You would unless you use the blood of the correct creatures . . . blood that ages so slowly that even a fast-healing body like yours won't recognize it as dead and feel the need to get rid of it right away."

"The blood of gods . . ." said Hildr.

"Would be ideal, but good luck cornering Thor or any of the other Aesir or Vanir gods. No, you need something a little more accessible. You need the blood of elves."

Gunnr laughed.

"What's so funny?" said Gunnhild.

"You said more accessible and then suggest we use elf blood. You know that as Valkyries, we can only transport between Midgard, Valhalla, and Helheim?" Gunnr said.

"You can use a Bifrost key," said Gunnhild.

"Do you have one?"

"No. . . ."

"There you have it," said Gunnr turning to Hildr. "This rune writer you've brought us is of no use. She cannot draw the runic tattoos we need and suggests impossible solutions. What now, sister?"

"How many elves would it take?" said Hildr.

"Less blood runs through their veins and there are three of you, plus I will need extra to do some experiments first. Maybe five to ten."

Hildr turned to face Gunnr.

"What are you thinking, sister?" said Gunnr.

"I think . . . I have an idea."

WHO ARE YOU ANGRY AT

Thyra and Helga returned to the main road once Sleipnir was fully loaded and well-fed. They trotted along in silence as the sun inched higher into the morning sky. Helga observed her surroundings, taking in everything with the mild amazement that a newborn takes in their surroundings. Thyra watched her.

"This is all new to you, isn't it?" she said.

Helga shifted her gaze towards Thyra.

"It is, and it is not. It is a strange feeling knowing something exists and yet finally seeing it for the first time. Have you ever spent this much time on the mainland?"

"No," said Thyra. "Most of my life has been on the island. On occasion, I would come to Borgarnes, but it would not be for long."

"So, this is all new to you too."

"Sure. I guess it is."

"You do not seem to be so enthused?"

"You're inside my head. You know why."

"I'm not inside your head, I was just born of you, and I said we would drift apart."

"I did not think it would be so quick."

"What bothers you about this land?"

"The people," said Thyra. "They fear and hate me, yet they do not know me."

"I see."

"They would laugh at me and say terrible things, and don't get me wrong . . . I'm not so soft that their words could ever break me . . . but their irrational hatred towards me makes me angry. But this time . . ."

"This time what?"

Thyra looked over at the hovering flygja.

"This time, they did go too far. The owner . . . former owner of this horse, killed my father . . . or at least tried to until those Valkyries saved him . . . saved him? They ended up killing him themselves."

"That is tragic."

"It's worse than tragic."

"Who are you angriest at?" said Helga.

"I don't know. Everyone."

"It's a simple question."

"Without a simple answer," said Thyra.

"There are four parties involved with the death of your father. The bigoted humans, the Valkyries, your father himself, and you. So, I ask you again . . . who are you angriest at?"

"Enough, Helga. I was supposed to be on this journey alone."

"I'll be quiet for now, but I'm always here."

"Hmph."

Thyra turned away from Helga and looked forward. The sun was up now, and the few clouds in the sky did nothing to provide shade. But despite that, the cool winter air was quite chilling, and the wind did not help. With one hand, Thyra pulled her pelt tighter. She was still hours away from Mímisbrunnr and Mimir, who resided at the top of the mountain.

Sleipnir trotted along. Helga levitated to the right of Thyra and Sleipnir, just out of view.

"This will be a cold one," said Helga under her breath.

"It's always a cold one," said Thyra.

"Oh, but not like this. I can feel it in my bones. This will be a winter to remember, and it is only just getting started."

Thyra observed Helga questionably. How could this being who only just appeared and could not explain her origin know anything about the world of Midgard and the winter to come? She considered asking her to explain further but then did not want to hear it.

They continued in silence. An hour later, a man on horseback appeared on the horizon. Helga dropped to the ground and began to walk.

"Just get on the horse," said Thyra. "It'll look strange a young girl walking alongside me on horseback."

Helga looked up at Thyra and smiled. She immediately climbed onto Sleipnir and held onto Thyra around the waist. The man came near, and he locked eyes with Thyra. She could see the fear slip over him as he gazed upon a dark elf. He then looked at the young girl holding onto her, and Thyra could see the bewilderment enter his eyes.

His mouth began to open, but before he spoke, he kicked his heels into his horse's flank and shouted, "Yah." Not before long, he was gone.

"He feared you and was concerned for me, but not concerned enough to do or at least say anything," said Helga.

"Typical human cowardice."

"That must get old," said Helga.

"You have no idea."

FIFTEEN

A DINNER PARTY

200 Years Ago: Svartalfheim

Hagen stood in the kitchen of the cottage he shared with his new wife, watching through the window as Ase trained the young boy who lived next door. His name was Hakon. The two dueled. Ase was casually parrying Hakon's attacks, barely breaking a sweat, while Hakon was breathing heavily, trying to keep up with his teacher.

"Think of the sword as an extension of yourself, Hakon," said Ase as she parried another of his attacks. "You're trying to force the sword to act. Just let it flow."

He swung the sword, and Ase countered, knocking the blade from the boy's hand.

"I give up," said Hakon.

"Don't give up. You're just starting. Let us take a break."

Hakon nodded and wiped the sweat from his brow. Ase turned to face her husband, who was watching and smiling. She smiled back and chuckled a little.

Hagen appeared in the backyard, holding a tray with various snacks. He set it down on a table next to Hakon and Ase.

"How are your parents?" he said to Hakon.

"They're ok. They are hoping I will be a great swordsman so I can protect my little sister since there is a war going on."

"That war isn't coming to Svartalfheim," said Ase. "The Aesir and the Vanir gods are just having a temper tantrum. It'll blow over."

"I don't know, love," said Hagen. "They're saying fighting has already spilled into Midgard. Hundreds of humans were killed at Nyköping by some rogue gods. That's what my mother told me."

"Svartalfheim is not Midgard," said Ase.

Hagen shrugged his shoulders and grabbed one of the snacks off the tray.

"My parents are worried," said Hakon. "They think the gods will turn against us."

"No offense Hakon but your parents have always been worried about everything. I have known your mom and dad for a long time. This is how they have always been," said Ase.

"You think we will be, ok?" Hakon said.

"I know we will," said Ase.

"My wife . . . the eternal optimist," said Hagen.

"Do you agree with Hakon's parents?"

"I don't know. It cannot hurt to be a little vigilant. These are unprecedented times. The gods have never mobilized on this scale before."

"All right. Breaks over. Come on, Hakon, let's get back to it then. If the gods show up wanting to fight, we'll give them one."

Hakon grabbed his sword and returned to the center of the backyard. Ase kissed her husband and met Hakon on the faux battlefield.

An hour later, Hakon and Ase finished up their training session.

"Remember to tell Tove and Geir to bring over little Saga. We have not seen her since she was born," said Ase as she put her sword away.

"I will," Hakon said. "They may want to come over this evening if that is ok with you."

"Of course, it is. We'll have dinner prepared."

Hakon smiled and sheathed his sword.

"Thank you for the lesson," he said and took off down the road.

Ase watched the young boy run off and then headed back inside her cottage.

"He's going to be quite the swordsman one day," said Hagen.

"Yeah . . . one day," said Ase. "He's got a kind soul. But his parents might be reaching for the stars if they think being a warrior is in his future. He is smart, though. Very smart. Should probably be a scholar."

Hagen laughed, "I thought a boy's teacher was supposed to have faith?"

"I have faith . . . that maybe he should try something else."

"Maybe we can talk to his parents about that tonight at dinner."

"He's their child. Maybe we can raise our own to be a scholar one day," said Ase.

Hagen reached out and grabbed her hand.

"We should start," he said.

"If we do, they'll have your gift. We'll need your mother to help; she is hard to reach."

"You know she had to disappear once the war broke out. She keeps in touch, but—"

"I know . . ."

"I don't want her to risk coming out of hiding to see her future grandchild."

Ase nodded in agreement.

"The power your mother has . . . what she is . . . what you are . . . our child will surely be the same. If your mother won't be around, then you will have to teach them, and you have barely mastered your abilities."

"You know I'm practicing," said Hagen.

"Not enough. You're as skilled with your abilities as that boy is with a sword," said Ase.

"I don't want to draw too much attention to our family," he said.

"If your mother is not going to be around, then you need to learn more about this thing inside of you because if we have a child, then you will need to guide them. Do you understand?"

Hagen looked at the ground.

"I know," he said.

"Not today but this week, you need to start honing this power. I train with a sword every day; you need to do the same . . . with whatever it is you have."

Hagen nodded. Ase gently kissed him on the lips.

"Good," she said.

That evening, Hakon led his parents into Hagen and Ase's home. Tove was holding baby Saga, and Geir carried a small bag with the baby's food.

"It smells wonderful in here," said Tove as she crossed the threshold into the home.

"Welcome," said Ase. "The food is almost finished. We have mead and tea, whichever you like."

Drinks in hand, the families migrated into the primary room of the cottage, where a fire was roaring. It warmed the entire home and kept the cold of winter at bay.

"Hakon says you are a tough teacher," Tove said.

"Does he?" replied Ase while looking at the boy.

He had an awkward smile spread across his face.

"That's good. Be tough on him. That is why we wanted you to train him. You're the best fighter in Svartalfheim."

"I push him when I need to," said Ase.

Hagen entered the room holding mead for Geir and tea for Tove. They took the beverages. Geir took a sip, but Tove sat hers down next to her.

"Thank you," they both said.

Hagen sat by Hakon.

"The food will be ready soon," he said.

"So how has having a newborn in the home been treating you?" said Ase.

Tove laughed.

"It's an adventure."

"To be fair, she is calmer than Hakon was when he was her age," said Geir.

"That's true. Hakon was a stinker," said Tove.

Hakon looked up at his parents, who were overtly talking bad about him.

"I was not that bad," he said.

"How would you know Mr. drops-food-just-to-make-us-pick-it-up," said Geir.

The same awkward smile spread across Hakon's face a second time.

"What about you two?" said Tove. "When are you going to be parents?"

"That's a good question. But soon, I suspect," answered Ase. "Hagen's mother gifted us a Bifrost key when we got married, so we were able to travel the nine realms, which was amazing, but we are getting ready for the next stage of life."

"That's great. Saga will have someone to play with since Hakon is too busy lately," said Tove.

"Did I do something wrong before we came over here?" said Hakon.

"Sorry, son," laughed Tove.

The whole room joined in her laughter. Hakon rolled his eyes at his parents, who seemed to be taking too much pleasure at his expense. Hagen looked over his shoulder at the stove.

"Ok, I think dinner is ready."

An hour later, the two families finished their meal and were wrapping up a beautiful evening.

"I'm glad we did this," said Hagen.

"We're glad you had us over. The food was fantastic," said Tove.

"Ase, I was talking to Iona this afternoon and told her you're training Hakon. She mentioned that she might also ask you to train her daughter, Hillevi. Would that be ok if she joined Hakon tomorrow?"

"The more, the merrier," said Ase. "I have extra swords if she needs one."

"Fantastic. I will let her know. She will probably stop by just to say thank you. I think this war between the gods has her a bit stirred up. It's got me stirred up. I know that."

"I don't think we have anything to worry about in Svartalfheim," said Ase.

"Easy for you to say," said Tove with a smile. "You're a better fighter than any god."

"I don't know about that," laughed Ase. "But I appreciate the kind words."

"Anyway, I will let Iona know about Hillevi. Take care."

"Thank you for the food," said Hakon before following his mother and sister out the front door.

"Take care," said Geir. "We'll host the next one."

Ase and Hagen stood in the doorway, watching the other family make their way down the road towards their own cottage.

"Nice family," said Hagen.

The following day, Hillevi joined Hakon for sword fighting lessons. She was naturally more skilled than Hakon, but the few lessons he had ahead of her matched them. That would change in time. But the two bonded quickly.

SIXTEEN

LOOKING INWARD

Helga held onto Thyra's waist as the two trotted along the dirt road. They had traveled for the last few hours in quiet and passed no one. This was no surprise, and a good thing, since they were now so far from the nearest town that if they did encounter humans, it would only be a wild band of Vikings.

Finally, Helga spoke up.

"What was it like growing up in Midgard?"

"Hmm?"

"The man we passed a way back got me thinking . . . what was it like for you to grow up in Midgard?"

"You're rather inquisitive."

"I can't be curious?"

"What do you and don't you know about me? Weren't you manifested by me? Shouldn't you know some of this stuff?"

"I'm just making conversation."

"I don't want to make conversation."

"Talking can be cathartic."

"And so can silence."

Helga sighed.

"It was fine," said Thyra.

"I'll leave it alone."

"Growing up in Midgard had its challenges. I was fortunate enough to be surrounded by people who loved me but being mostly confined to an island was less than ideal."

"Did you ever think of Svartalfheim?"

"Of course, I did. But I didn't think it was reachable."

"But now maybe it is."

"Now maybe it is."

"Your parents had a Bifrost key all this time. . . ."

"They did."

"And so now you can go," said Helga.

"There are still the Valkyries."

"And if you can do something about them?"

"Then, of course."

"If you go to Svartalfheim, you'll get to see where you come from . . . where your parents come from . . . your blood parents."

"Are you trying to make a point?"

"Just conversation."

"Hmph."

The silence returned as the duo reached the crest of a hilltop, and a small mountain surrounded by a dense forest appeared in the distance. Thyra stopped the horse and took out the map.

"That is Mímisbrunnr," she said, pointing at the small mountain.

Sleipnir started moving again, and Helga returned to the conversation.

"I don't blame you if you don't want to go down that path, but understanding who you are is important," said Helga.

"Have I stated that I don't want to know who I am? What are you getting at?"

"Sorry, I don't mean to be pushy. This is an inward-facing thing—I'm just voicing it."

"Well, don't. It's getting irritating."

"I'll stop."

"You look like a child, but you are clearly not one," she whispered.

Helga looked up at her and smiled.

"I'm here to help you; sometimes, the help people need is overcoming internal barriers."

"Noted," said Thyra.

The silence returned as they descended the hill and entered the dense forest. Sunlight struggled to reach the forest floor and lit a patchwork of spots on the ground in rays.

Thyra could feel a subtle tickle on her fingertips and at the base of her neck. She rubbed her fingers together and touched her neck.

"Are you ok?" asked Helga.

"I feel strange, as if there is something all around us. It is not unfamiliar. Do you feel it?"

"Just barely," she said.

Sleipnir trotted onward.

The forest grew denser and darker as they moved towards the small mountain. It was midday, but underneath the canopy, it was starting to feel like night. It was colder too—much colder. Thyra pulled her pelt in tightly with one hand and held the reins with the other. Not before long, they reached the base of the mountain.

Thyra stopped the horse and looked up. She saw something flash over the mountain. It was a bird of some sort, but she could not be clear of what kind. She looked back at Helga.

"I saw it," she said.

"We need to be cautious as we approach. I know nothing of Mimir," said Thyra.

"I will be vigilant."

Thyra pulled on the reins, and Sleipnir began the slow ascent up the side of the mountain.

THE BROTHER OF THE BUILDER

Hildr looked at her two sisters, who were now covered head to toe in runic drawings, tattoos made of rare ash and their blood.

"You look like you could take on the Aesir," she said.

"I feel like it," said Gunnr.

"Are you ready?" said Gunnhild to Hildr.

Hildr nodded and turned to follow Gunnhild. Gunnr placed a hand on her shoulder. Hildr looked back at her sister.

"Our faith in you is strong," she said.

Hildr placed her hand over Gunnhild's.

"We are almost there."

One Year Ago

Hlaðguðr waited in a mighty hall, well-lit with torches and well-decorated with paintings of glorious battles. She did not know why he summoned her, but it did not matter. He who summoned her was never questioned.

A door to her left opened. Her attention shot towards it. It remained open for a second, but no one entered. Her anticipation built but then appeared a small man in a robe. A sword hung by his side. Hlaðguðr could tell it did not get much use.

"I am sorry to keep you waiting," he said.

"Hermod," said Hlaðguðr. "I was not expecting you."

"No. I am sure you were not. I'm afraid the Allfather will not be able to meet with you today. He sent me instead to deliver his message."

Hlaðguðr tried her best to hide her disappointment.

Hermod approached her. She stood up out of respect as the minor Aesir god neared.

"Please have a seat. I will make this quick."

Hlaðguðr sat back down.

"Valkyries such as yourself are a fine specimen. Very capable. Very powerful, and you are one of the best. That is why Odin has entrusted you with this special mission."

"I'm ready," said Hlaðguðr. "Whatever he needs. I will do it."

"He knows you will."

Hours Later

Hlaðguðr arrived at the edge of the river Ilfing. She sprouted her powerful wings and lifted into the air. The river never froze and ran swiftly. No boats crossed it; for most, it was the proper barrier between Asgard and Jotunheim. But for the daring and those who could fly, it was only a challenge to overcome.

Hlaðguðr hovered for a moment, then began her flight over the river, looking down at the rushing water. She had never crossed into Jotunheim before. For her entire life, she had served as a Midgardian Valkyrie. But when Odin has a special mission for you, you do it, no questions asked. The water was fierce but not a concern for her from her place in the air.

Minutes later, she touched down on the other side, in a different realm. The realm of Jotunheim. Hlaðguðr looked back across the river. For all she knew, this was one of the only places in all the nine realms where one could travel between realms without a Bifrost.

"There must be something magical about the river," she whispered.

"There is," said a deep, bellowing voice.

Hlaðguðr turned around, startled. Standing before her was a mighty giant, wielding a club larger than her entire body, wings included. She looked up at the creature.

"Who are you?" she said defiantly.

The giant turned its big face down towards her and grinned.

"I am the brother of the builder," he said. "My name is Endre."

"Well, Endre, you're the one I have come to see. I was sent to retrieve what you stole from the Allfather. Hand it over, and I won't be forced to hurt you."

"You hurt me? Do not make me laugh puny Valkyrie. You are in Jötunheim now. The realm of the giants. If you're lucky, maybe I won't break every bone in your body and send you back to Asgard crippled."

Hlaðguðr formed a fist with one hand and placed the other on the hilt of her sword. Endre's grin widened.

"You were waiting for the Allfather, were you not?" said Hlaðguðr.

"That I was," said Endre.

"Then you are not the only one disappointed by his absence today."

She unsheathed her weapon and launched at the giant. Endre stumbled backward, shifting his weight so he could swing the mighty club. But she was fast and nimble. He was slow and brutish. She avoided his first and second strike, deflected the third, and sliced the giant across his chest. Blood spurt from the open wound, washing over her.

She cleared her eyes and saw the giant retreating.

"You will return what you stole from the Allfather today," she shouted and chased after him.

Endre's giant steps were powerful and shook the ground as he ran. He lept over pools of water that smaller creatures would have had to swim through. Hlaðguðr pursued him through the air. Her mighty wings flapping gracefully, propelling her forward.

"It was supposed to be Him that showed up, not you," shouted Endre as he ran. "The Aesir gods killed my brother. My quarrel is with the Gallows God and his bastard of a son Thor."

"Today, your quarrel is with me," Hlaðguðr shouted back.

"So be it," whispered the giant.

He pivoted on his right heel, kicked dirt into the air, and dropped into a massive hole in the ground. Just like that, he was out of view.

"What?" said Hlaðguðr.

She slowed and then stopped her pursuit, scanning the horizon for the giant who somehow evaded her, despite his size.

"This is not your realm," said Endre, his voice emanating from everywhere and nowhere simultaneously.

Hlaðguðr spun in 360 degrees.

"Where are you?" she shouted.

"I'm here," he said.

His free hand rose from the ground beneath her and gripped her tightly. She squirmed within his grasp, but it was to no avail. She may have been faster, but he was so much stronger.

"Let. Me. Go," she said.

Endre emerged from the dirt, his face covered in sweat and mud. His chest was bloodied and covered in dirt and debris.

"The Aesir gods think that the nine realms are theirs to play with and that the lives of other creatures are beneath them. My brother offered to build a wall to protect Asgard, and they killed him for his work. I try to lure Odin here to exact my revenge, and he sends a lone Valkyrie. You should know he probably knew it was a trap and sent you to spring it."

Hlaðguðr continued to squirm in Endre's grasp. He tightened his grip, and she let out a deep, guttural scream as the bones in her arms snapped.

"Free me, you bastard," she shouted. "Let me go."

Endre gritted his teeth. His ominous grin turned to a frown.

"I must admit. I can understand the pleasure Odin must take in toying with creatures he thinks are lesser."

Endre tightened his grip further, and the bones in her thighs snapped.

"Valkyries heal quickly, do they not?"

He eased his grip, and almost immediately, he could feel her body trying to heal and the bones coming together. Then he squeezed tightly again the bones which had partially healed, started to splinter—shards of bone pierce the muscle that housed them.

The Valkyrie had never felt a pain like this and passed out. Endre laughed and tossed her body to the ground. Other giants appeared alongside Endre and around Hlaðguðr.

"This is what the Allfather thinks of us," said Endre to his brethren. "They send a Valkyrie, a messenger, an errand runner to do his bidding. We shall send him a message back."

One Day Later

Hermod waited at the edge of Ilfing for Hlaðguðr's return. This mission of hers was not to take more than a few hours. He tapped his foot as his patience waned.

"Where is she?" he whispered.

Just then, something caught his eye, and he looked up to see something flying across the river. His face turned puzzled since it was not the Valkyrie flying at him.

"What is that?" he whispered.

Before he could work out what it was, it landed on his side of the Ilfing with a thud and rolled to his feet. It was a cream-colored sack. He knelt to inspect the sack's contents, but before he opened it, he heard a voice shouting at him.

He looked up and saw a giant standing on the other side of the Ilfing.

"Asgard is on borrowed time."

Hermod grimaced at Endre's words and opened the sack. What he saw made him fall over. Then he heard the laughter of Endre.

Present

Hildr emerged from the hall, covered in the runic tattoos drawn by Gunnhild.

"Let's remember why we are doing this. Odin does not care about us. He sends us to fight and die for him for no reason. That changes today. With our increased and combined power, we can find that dark elf anywhere in Midgard."

E I G H T E E N

MIMIR

Thyra and Helga ascended the mountain that led to Mímisbrunnr. It was a steep incline, but Sleipnir handled it like a champion. Thyra was starting to wonder if the horse was Odin's eight-legged horse. She rubbed the back of its head.

"You're doing great," she said.

The cold would not let up. It felt like it was getting colder. Winter was here, and it was a fierce one.

"Mimir is something different from every creature in the nine realms, including the gods," said Helga.

"How do you know?"

"I don't know how I know, but I do know that is a fact."

"You are bizarre," said Thyra with a half-smile.

"I think I have some sort of connection to the World Tree. It clues me on certain things . . . something like that. I don't know."

Something caught Thyra's eye. She looked upward, having just missed whatever it was.

"Something is up there. I don't know what it is, but I've seen it twice now."

"Where?"

"Above the top of the mountain. It is flying overhead. I can't make it out entirely, though."

"Does it feel ominous?" said Helga.

91

"I can't tell."

"Then you know it doesn't feel good."

Sleipnir carried the duo up the mountain, and not before long, they were looking at a sea of treetops. This was the highest point Thyra had ever been, and she was amazed at the view of Midgard from this new vantage point. Midgard seemed so big and expansive and yet small all the same. She pulled on the reins to stop the horse and just gazed for a moment.

"Beautiful," she whispered.

"One of nine," said Helga.

"What?"

"Wait until you see them all," said Helga.

"Do you think I will?"

"Elves live a long time."

"When I was younger, I dreamed of exploring Midgard, but Dad warned against it. He said there were too many monsters in the world. I always thought he was referring to trolls and wolves, but he meant people. He kept me on the island for most of my childhood. That was until he lost his sister and her family. Then he did not let me out of his sight, and I joined him on his missions to the mainland to sell the family's mead. I do wonder who I would be if I had been allowed to explore more freely when I was younger."

"You're discovering that person now," said Helga. "The world will build a wall around you. Even those with the best intentions may inadvertently imprison you."

Thyra took in the view of Midgard for a few more seconds, then pulled on the reins of Sleipnir and continued their ascent.

"I'm told Mimir is the wisest in the land, but maybe it's you."

Helga laughed, "Hardly. But thank you."

Thyra and Helga did the rest of the climb in relative quiet. Conversations would start and stop, but the two did not discuss anything substantive. It was primarily idle talk to pass the time as they approached the mountain's peak. It was not long until they heard another voice, faint against the fierce wind.

"You made it," said the voice.

Thyra stopped Sleipnir. She and Helga looked around the top of the mountain.

"Where are you?" said Thyra.

"Over here," said the voice.

Thyra and Helga looked in the speaker's direction and saw a massive tree, partially hollowed out about three feet off the ground.

"In here."

The two women approached cautiously.

"I don't see you," said Thyra.

"I'm in the tree."

"In the tree?" Thyra whispered.

She walked up to the opening, gesturing for Helga to stand behind her.

"Let me see," said Helga.

"Just stay behind me."

Thyra leaned into the opening, then jumped back, startled.

"What?" said Helga.

"Would you give me a hand?" said the voice.

"How is this possible?" said Thyra.

She regained her nerve, reached into the tree, and pulled out a severed human head.

"Woh," said Helga.

"Are you Mimir?" said Thyra.

"In the flesh."

"What are you? What sort of magic is this?" said Thyra as she stepped away from the tree holding Mimir's head.

"I am a man. The wisest man alive," said Mimir. "And this is powerful . . . very powerful seidr magic. The kind that only the gods possess. One god in particular."

"Odin?" said Helga.

"I would nod if I could. But yes. The Allfather himself put me here."

"Why?"

"That, my friend, is a long story. But the abridged one is . . . he is spiteful."

"Mimir, we have traveled a great distance to speak with you because I was told you would provide the wisdom I need."

"Well, I am the wisest man alive. Did I not just say that?"

"What do the Valkyries want? And how do you defeat them?" said Thyra.

"I see. So, it's you."

"Do you know me?" said Thyra.

"I knew your parents. They said you would visit me one day. I did not want to assume. You're not the only dark elf in Midgard though you are rare."

"There are others in this realm?"

"Stay focused," said Helga.

"Right. About the Valkyries . . . what can you tell me about them? I want to know their weaknesses . . . what do they want the Bifrost key for? What is going on?"

"Do you see that stump behind you?" said Mimir.

Thyra and Helga turned around. There was a felled tree and a remaining stump.

"Place me on it and take a seat. Normally I request some form of payment, but your parents were good people, and to say what happened to the dark elves was tragic would be to put things extremely lightly. Therefore, I will tell you a story. It involves your parents, the Aesir gods, and a light elf named Volund the Smith. And trust me, it all connects to the Valkyries who pursue you."

NINETEEN

THE FIRST ASSAULT ON SVARTALFHEIM

200 Years Ago

Hakon and Hillevi sparred with one another as Ase watched them. Hillevi's natural talent was starting to show, but Hakon was determined to keep up. Ase secretly felt for the boy. He would never fight like either of them despite his parent's wishes. That did not mean she would not help him improve. Who knew . . . maybe he could surprise her?

But just as she had that thought, Hillevi knocked Hakon to his feet. Ase rolled her eyes, then ran over.

"Enough. Take a break."

She extended a hand and pulled Hakon to his feet.

"Remember, you must be like water. Flow, don't fight. Flow."

"I know, I know. It's just hard."

"All good things are difficult at first," said Hillevi.

"That's easy for you to say. You have been practicing less time, and you're already beating me."

"People learn and improve at their own pace," said Ase.

"And others choose different paths," added Hillevi.

"Enough," said Ase.

"She's right. Maybe I'm just not cut out for this."

"Keep working at it. We'll get you there," said Ase. "Let's go eat now, though."

The two kids smiled and followed Ase inside her home.

"Where has Hagen been lately?" said Hakon. "He has not been here the last two times I've come over to train."

"I was wondering the same," said Hillevi.

"He is training too," said Ase as she pulled a pot off the wood fire stove.

"With swords? Why wouldn't he train with you?" Hakon said.

"Not with swords. Hagen has a special power inside of him he inherited from his mother. He doesn't quite know how to control it, so he goes to the forest to train."

"What kind of power?" said Hillevi.

"That is what he is figuring out," said Ase as she situated a bowl in front of the child.

Just then, the door to the cottage crashed open. Hagen was standing in it, his face beaded with sweat. He was breathing heavy, having just run the whole way home. Ase, Hakon, and Hillevi turned to him, all extremely startled.

"What's going on?" shouted Ase.

"Hakon, Hillevi . . . where are your parents?" said Hagen frantically.

"I don't know . . . the market maybe," said Hakon.

"Same. I think," said Hillevi.

"We need to go get them and your siblings now."

"What is happening?" said Ase.

An explosion shook the cottage. Hagen turned around in the doorway and saw their home's yard and part of their neighbor's cottage going up in flames.

"The war is here," he said. "Grab the Bifrost key."

Ase and Hagen led. Hillevi and Hakon followed. The foursome navigated the burning streets of Gedser, their hometown in Svartalfheim. The market was on the far side of town, opposite the location of Ase and Hagen's home. The streets were burning. Smoke was rising high into the sky. Dark elves were scrambling to find safety.

"Who is attacking?" shouted Ase over the chaos. "The Aesir? The Vanir?"

"Neither," shouted Hagen. "It's the light elves."

"The light elves?" said Ase in disbelief. "Why would they . . . ?"

An explosion stopped the group in their tracks. Hakon and Hillevi fell backward. Ase and Hagen scrambled to pick them up.

"Come on, you two, we're almost there," said Ase.

"I'm scared," said Hillevi.

"It'll be ok," said Hakon.

He grabbed her hand.

The sky was dark with the thick, black smoke of burning homes, blocking the sun. Terrifying screams created a chorus of horror in all directions.

Another explosion tore apart a building to the right of Hagen, Ase, Hakon, and Hillevi. From the wreckage poured out two men and a child. They were shrieking as their bodies burned.

"Don't look," shouted Hagen.

Hagen and Ase ran to extinguish the flames, but they were too late. The three dark elves fell over in the dirt, their bodies contributing to the smoke clouds that covered Gedser.

Hakon and Hillevi stared, despite Hagen's instruction. Their bodies were trembling.

"Is that going to happen to us?" whispered Hillevi.

"No," said Hakon. "It's not. We are going to find your parents and get somewhere safe."

Ase and Hagen used their pelts to extinguish the flames of the two burning men and the one small child, but it was too little too late. The screams stopped long before they extinguished the flames. Ase continued to beat down what fire remained, but Hagen grabbed her arm and stopped her. She looked at him. He shook his head.

"We have to go."

She nodded in agreement; a small tear formed.

"Come on, kids. Let's get out of here," she said.

The market was in no better condition than any other part of Gedser. It was worse. From their vantage point, Hagen, Ase, Hakon, and Hillevi could see light elf soldiers slaughtering dark elves in the streets. The rain of fire had stopped, and the troops were moving in to clean up.

Hagen could see a woman hiding and two light elf soldiers approaching her. Unbeknownst to her, part of her pelt was exposed. As far as he could tell, she was the last surviving dark elf at the market. The soldiers removed the crate she had taken refuge behind, and she started to scream. Hagen covered the eyes of Hakon and Hillevi as the soldiers tied a rope around the woman's neck and hanged her from a shop sign. Her legs were kicking and her body was flailing as life escaped her.

"We have to find your parents and siblings now," said Hagen. "Ase stay with them. I'll scout for their families."

"Be safe."

"We should stick together," said Hakon.

"No. If something happens to me, you need to stay with Ase."

"But our families . . ." said Hillevi.

"He will find them," said Ase.

"Take them to the cave just outside of town where we first met years ago. I will find you there . . . with their families."

Hagen stood up slightly, still staying low to hide from unwanted onlookers.

"Hagen," said Ase.

"What?"

"Have you been practicing?"

He nodded, then leaped over the barrier the group was hidden behind and ran to the nearest building, taking care not to get caught. The screams of those being slaughtered had not subsided, which perversely, was a good thing because it meant there were still survivors. But the time between screams was growing, meaning folks were dwindling.

Hagen paused at the building for a second, scanned his surroundings, made sure he could move again, and took off towards the next closest building. The market was near.

The sky over Gedser was black at this point. The entire town was burning, and light elf soldiers were roaming the streets. Hagen stuck to the shadows and navigated as cautiously as he could.

His focus was on finding Tove, Geir, Saga, Iona, Kare, and Jarl, but in the back of his mind, he was wondering what could have compelled the light elves to attack. Their two realms had never been at odds, and the Great War was between the Aesir and Vanir gods. It was not a war for the other realms. It was just background noise for most realms. What changed?

The market was only feet away, and five light elf soldiers were standing aimlessly. They had their weapons sheathed, but regardless, blood covered their pelts. Hagen waited to make sure it was just the five, and it is a good thing he did because from just out of sight appeared one more. He was taller than the rest, and his pelt was more ornamental. He carried a spear, not a sword like the rest, and as soon as he appeared, the five aimless light elves became attentive. It was clear to Hagen that this one was in charge.

The leader and the five others exchanged words. Then the five dispersed, heading in different directions around the market. The screaming, which Hagen had not noticed had ceased, started up again.

"Please be alive," Hagen whispered. "Please."

Ase, Hillevi, and Hakon navigated the deserted streets and alleyways of Gedser, paying close attention to the movements of light elf soldiers. The edge of town was in sight, but two soldiers blocked their path. The three waited, hidden behind a building.

"Can we go around?" said Hillevi.

Ase scanned their surroundings. She shook her head.

"We'll be in the open anywhere but this way."

"What do we do?" said Hakon.

"I'm thinking."

"Ase they're coming."

The two soldiers started approaching. They were strolling, clearly not searching for anything or anyone, but they were about to be surprised.

"We are going to have to fight," said Ase.

"We can't fight," said Hakon.

"Yes, we can. Haven't we been training?" said Ase.

"But I'm no good. I can't do it."

"I agree with him. I don't feel ready for this," said Hillevi.

"We don't have time for you to feel ready. I will lead, and you two stay behind me. They'll be on us shortly."

"I'm scared," said Hillevi.

Ase knelt by the young girl.

"So am I."

Hagen maneuvered his way through the market, making sure not to run into any of the five light elves who were also making their way through the market. He especially made a point of avoiding the one in charge.

"Where are you?" he whispered.

A loud crash caught his attention. He saw a man and woman get up and run as one of the five light elves approached their position. The light elf quickly cut them down.

"These guys are faster and stronger than any light elf I've ever seen," whispered Hagen. "Are they all like that or just these ones?"

He continued, but now even more cautiously. Through the market, he moved cautiously but with as much haste as he could muster. He searched until he heard someone whisper his name. Then he stopped and looked behind him.

Iona, Kare, and Jarl were hiding in an underground passageway. The door was slightly ajar, and he could see their eyes looking back at him.

Iona waved him over.

"I'm going to get you out of here. Is Hakon's family with you?"

Tears formed in Iona's eyes.

"Just Saga. It all happened so fast. Jarl was carrying Saga. Geir and Tove were ahead of us all. As soon as the light elves attacked, we hid immediately," she whispered. "There was nothing we could do." She started to weep more intensely.

"It's ok. It's ok. We need to get you out of here now, though."

"How?" said Kare. "These things are everywhere. They're fast."

"They're just light elves," said Hagen. "Soldiers, sure. But we can make it if we run."

"They're not just soldiers. They're unnatural. We've seen too many try to run. As soon as they do, those five are on them so fast they don't know what hit them," said Iona as she dried her tears.

Hagen thought back to the man and woman he saw attempting to flee.

"Ase, Hillevi, and Hakon are escaping the town. There is a cave just beyond the edge of Gedser. Do you know it?"

"Yes," said Iona.

"When I say run. I want you to go straight there. I'll hold them off until you're clear, then I will catch up."

"That's impossible," said Iona. "That's suicide."

Hagen's eyes glowed red.

"When I say. Run. Don't worry about me."

Ase clashed swords with the two light elf soldiers. Hillevi and Hakon stayed behind her as she held her own. The soldiers were fearsome, but it was clear why she was their instructor. She parried over and over. She would take a step forward, then take a step back. Her and the two soldiers were locked in a stalemate.

Hagen put some distance between himself and where he found Iona, Kare, Jarl, and Saga. Then red energy started to swirl around his hands. He stood up and immediately caught the attention of the five light elf soldiers roaming through the market. In unison, they shifted their gaze towards him.

"Hopefully, that practice wasn't all for nothing."

The first of the soldiers leaped at him. Hagen raised his right hand and unleashed a near-blinding blast of the red light. It caught the elf by surprise and sent him flying across the market hall. The others all looked at one another curiously.

"You can do this," he whispered to himself.

"We can help," said Hakon to Hillevi, noticing Ase's inability to get a leg up on the soldiers she was fighting.

"How?" said Hillevi.

"See that building?" he said, pointing to a two-story cottage to their right. "We can ambush them from there."

Hillevi nodded.

"Let's do it."

Inside the cottage, Hillevi found a bunch of heavy cookware.

"We can use this," she said.

Ase noticed the two run off, as did the soldiers. The soldiers tried to break away from their engagement with Ase, but she did not let them. She kept the battle contained in the street while Hakon and Hillevi gained leverage.

The battle between Hagen and the five light elf soldiers was in full swing. They would attack, but his inherited magic would deflect anything they would throw at him. He did not even need a weapon. This power he had was all he needed, and thank goodness he had spent time honing his skills.

As the battle continued, Iona, Kare, Jarl, and Saga slowly climbed out of the hole in the ground they were hiding in. One by one, they made their escape. They kept low to avoid being seen and headed towards the rear of the market, opposite where Hagen was fighting the five light elves. Next to them was a blacksmith shop. Kare grabbed a sword for himself and Iona.

"Take Saga, Jarl." She said, handing the baby to the young boy.

Kare handed Iona one of the swords he found. The family kept on moving.

"Where do you think you're going?" said a deep voice.

The family was caught. They turned around and stared face to face with the larger, more ornate light elf who wielded the spear. Iona and Kare shifted in front of the two children.

"Let us go," said Iona.

"Tell your friend to stop fighting."

Iona and Kare looked at one another and subtly nodded.

"Jarl, run," said Kare.

He hesitated.

"Run," shouted Iona.

The ornate light elf smirked.

"Fool."

The first of the soldiers to be hit by cookware was also the first to be beaten by Ase. The distraction was brief but effective, and she placed her sword through his abdomen. The second, recognizing that he was beaten without his partner, started to scream for help, but Ase pounced. She quickly got the upper hand and placed her arm around his neck. He squirmed, but soon enough, he was unconscious in her grasp. Hillevi and Hakon ran back downstairs to join her in the street.

"Why didn't you . . ." Hillevi started.

"Kill him?" said Hakon, finishing Hillevi's thought.

"We need to know what is going on here," said Ase. "He might be our best chance at figuring that out."

Ase picked up the soldier and threw him over her shoulder.

"Let's go," she said. "We must hurry."

"No," shouted Iona as the ornate light elf stabbed his spear through Kare's chest, impaling the man against the market wall.

Hagen heard her yell and looked back. He saw the light elf holding Iona by the neck in one hand and Kare with the spear protruding from his chest. Hagen's eyes shot wide open.

"No," he whispered.

Hagen quickly pivoted and ran over to help his friends. The ornate light elf turned around as he approached, flung Iona, and pulled the spear from Kare. His body thudded as it hit the ground.

Hagen's eyes were glowing bright red, and the energy emanated from his body was all around him. He charged the light elf, but the five he was fighting were not beat yet and came running after him. With a blinding light, Hagen batted them away without even looking. They went flying in all directions—some even through the roof of the market. At that moment, the expression on the ornate light elf's face went from surprised to impressed.

"That was different," he said; a rainbow shone down around him, and he was gone.

The energy around Hagen dissipated, and he scurried over to Iona.

"Are you ok?" he said, assisting her to her feet.

"That monster killed Kare. Who was he?"

"I don't know," answered Hagen somberly.

Ase sat her captive light elf soldier on the ground against the cave wall and shook him so he would wake. Hillevi and Hakon were standing nearby, each with swords drawn, but it was not them that struck fear into the soldier. It was Ase who was unarmed and at eye-level with him.

"Why are you doing this?" she said calmly.

The soldier started to breathe more heavily. He scanned back and forth between the two children.

"Don't look at them. Look at me. Why are the light elves attacking?"

He shifted his gaze to meet Ase.

"We . . . were ordered to," he said.

"By who?"

"I shouldn't be talking to you about this," he said. "He'll kill me."

"Who will? What is going on? Why are you here?" shouted Ase.

Just then, Ase heard Jarl and Saga making their way through the cave.

"Ase?" Jarl shouted.

"We're here," said Ase.

Ase saw Jarl almost drop Saga when he saw the light elf against the wall.

"What's going on here?" he said.

"Where is everyone else?" said Ase.

"They told me to take Saga and run."

Hillevi ran over and hugged her brother. Hakon approached also.

"I'll take her," he said, holding his arms out to grab his baby sister.

Jarl passed Saga to him.

"Where are my parents?"

Jarl did not immediately respond. His silence was all that Hakon needed. His eyes welled up, and tears started streaming down his face. Ase turned toward the boy and put her arms around him.

"I'm so sorry," she whispered repeatedly.

"Hagen was fighting. So were my parents. I don't know if they made it out."

"We're glad you're here," said Ase.

"Yes, Jarl. I'm happy you made it," said Hillevi.

"Hakon, will you be ok for a moment while I continue to question him," said Ase gesturing towards the light elf, who had remained still and simply observed the interactions between the dark elves.

Hakon nodded; Ase let go and turned back towards the light elf.

"We're not supposed to be involved in this war. It's a war between the Aesir and the Vanir, but we were recruited," said the light elf.

"Who recruited you?" said Ase.

"The Aesir," said the light elf.

"Odin?"

"Ase, Hakon, Hillevi," shouted Hagen as he entered the cave with Iona in tow. "Did Jarl and Saga make it?"

"They made it," said Ase.

Hagen and Iona caught up to the rest of the group. They eyed the light elf.

"Has he said anything?" said Hagen.

"Mom," said Jarl. "Where is Dad?"

And just like Jarl's silence before with Hakon, Iona's silence was all Jarl needed to know his father would never be with them again.

Iona wiped a tear away and hugged her son and daughter.

"What happened?" whispered Ase to Hagen.

"There was something different about the light elves at the market, and their leader was there too . . . I think he was their leader."

"He isn't," said the light elf.

Hagen and Ase turned their attention towards him.

"Who is he?" said Hagen.

"His name is Volund the Smith. He is an alchemist who uses rune writing and experimentation to alter creatures . . . those things you faced were some of his inventions."

"Alchemist?" said Ase.

"A term he learned from beyond the nine realms to describe his magic. I don't know everything he does, but I know it isn't natural," said the light elf.

"I've heard it before," said Hagen. "That is what my mother called it."

"What is it?" Ase said.

"It's an extremely specialized form of a seidr magic. It can manipulate the world to the extent of the wielder's creativity and skill. It's not like rune writing, where things can be enhanced, shifted, or changed on the surface. Alchemy changes things structurally. My mom tried showing me, but I could never grasp it. But you said something interesting. You said Volund learned this term beyond the nine realms?"

"That's what he said. I don't know what that means. I didn't know there are realms beyond the nine."

"There aren't . . . are there?" said Hagen.

"Hagen, you're missing the point of all this . . . why did Odin order the light elves to attack us?"

"I don't . . ."

At that moment, the rainbow that had teleported Volund away from the market, teleported him to the cave entrance. The light elf, who had until this moment been cooperative, jumped to his feet. He violently pushed Ase to the ground, causing her to tumble through a small hole in the cave floor. He started to run, but Hagen blasted him in the back, and he too fell to the cave floor.

He ran and turned the elf over.

"I'm sorry," said the light elf as the life passed from his eyes.

"I'm curious about your power," said Volund as he slowly passed through the cave towards the group of survivors. His five light elf creatures were walking behind him. "I recognize it, and yet it is still unique. I have not seen anything quite like it."

Hagen backed up slowly. So did the rest of his family, save for Ase, who was trying to pick herself from the hole where she had bounced off a small boulder and landed on her stomach.

"Stay behind me," said Hagen.

"If you come with me willingly, I will spare them," said Volund.

"A deal I could make if I knew you were telling the truth," replied Hagen.

Hagen noticed Hillevi and Hakon help Ase. They were struggling—she was heavier than she looked—but they managed to pick her up. She rested partially on their shoulders and limped backward to be with Hagen and Jarl.

The group inched away from Volund and his monsters, but the back of the cave was fast approaching.

"There is nowhere for you to run," said Volund. "You can take a chance with my offer, or you can all perish here and now. I can use your body for experimentation, dead or alive. I would rather not, but sometimes these things can't be helped."

"Tell us why the light elves are attacking," said Hagen. "And I will go with you."

"It was Thor's idea," said Volund.

"Thor?" said Hagen in disbelief.

Hagen noticed Ase unhook her arm from around Hillevi and pull something from her pocket. She switched the device to her other hand, which was still clinging around Hakon's shoulder.

"Put your hand on Hagen's back," she whispered to Hillevi.

Hillevi did as instructed. Iona caught on to what was happening and grabbed her son's hand.

As soon as they interlocked, Ase triggered the Bifrost key; a bright rainbow flash lit up the cave, and the family was gone.

"Hmph," said Volund.

The family touched down far away from Gedser, but they could see the smoke rising, and it was not just there. Looking out at the Svartalfheim horizon, they could see similar attacks in towns all over.

Hakon, Hillevi, Jarl, and Saga huddled around Ase, Hagen, and Iona as Svartalfheim burned. The three kids old enough to recognize what was happening all had tears in their eyes. On some base level, even Saga understood something terrible was happening. Hagen took Ase's hand and turned to her.

"Are you ok?" he whispered.

"I am," she said, then looked down. "What are we going to do?"

The fires of a burning Svartalfheim cast the survivors on the hilltop in an eerie yellow and orange glow. The Great War had arrived with devastating effects.

TWENTY

A HALL DIVIDED

"I found her," said Hildr as she, Gunnr, and Svipul used their combined power to scan Midgard for Thyra. "She is climbing the mountain of Mímisbrunnr. I guess she is smarter than we gave her credit for seeking out the wisdom of Mimir."

"Let us get there quickly to hear what he tells her. We can't attack there; otherwise, we'll surely get the attention of Odin, but we can get a jump on her next move and maybe even talk to Mimir ourselves," said Hildr.

Her sisters agreed with the plan.

"For six weeks, the light elves attacked Svartalfheim. And almost all of the dark elves were eradicated. It was a highly coordinated genocide—the single most devastating massacre in the history of the nine realms. The atrocities the light elves committed against the dark elves were . . . well, I dare not say. Your parents survived, but it would not be their last run-in with Volund. Years later, he would track them down and disrupt the community they were helping rebuild. However, your father had semi-mastered his abilities, and your mother had trained a new generation of warriors. But they knew Volund would not give up and would adapt, so they eventually fled to Midgard to draw his attention away from the healing dark elf community. But there are so few dark elves in the nine realms because of that first attack," said Mimir.

"Why did the light elves attack my people?" said Thyra.

"Early in the Great War, the Aesir gods realized that they were too evenly matched with the Vanir and that an edge was needed. Humans were briefly considered, but their society was not proficient enough in seidr magic to make a significant difference. Back then, there was no such thing as rune writers. The Aesir gods needed more, so they turned their attention to light elves, the second most proficient users of seidr magic besides dark elves. But Thor knew that if the Aesir recruited the light elves, the Vanir would recruit the dark elves to even the playing field, so he suggested they preempt that by wiping out the dark elves first. All the Aesir agreed with the suggestion except for Frigg, for which Odin banished her to Midgard. Ironically, Frigg's banishment to Midgard would be what led to humans becoming better users of seidr magic, but that is a story for a different time."

"My people were killed purely for strategic reasons to give the Aesir an advantage in a foolish war?"

"Sadly, yes," said Mimir.

"Why did the light elves agree to this? It wasn't their war."

"Odin promised them godhood. Ascension to the pantheon. Of course, this was a lie. The whole war with the Vanir war partially because there were two pantheons . . . Odin would never allow for a third. Eventually, the light elves would realize this and stop assisting the Aesir . . . but Volund . . . never stopped. His allegiance was never to the Aesir or even his own people . . . it was to himself, and he had seen a power in your father that he had to have. A power that exists in you."

"What is this power?" said Thyra.

"That, I do not know, and that is the absolute truth. I wish I did. But I don't think that is what is important."

"What could be more important than understanding this power?"

"What you do with it. The Valkyries who pursue you are running away from Odin, but they have been driven down a dark path. They have a human rune writer who will tattoo their bodies, so they'll be strong enough to survive the second Great War, but they need the blood of dark elves to make those tattoos stick since your people age so slowly and Valkyries heal so quickly. Your parents told me this much when they arrived in Midgard. They'd used a seeing rune to look as far into the future as possible to make sure things would be ok, and this is about how far they got."

"And with so few dark elves left . . ."

"They want to find the town your parents helped recreate in Svartalfheim. Two hundred years later, it is still getting its footing since dark elves reproduce so slowly. If those Valkyries have their way, it could mean the end for your people."

"What do I do now?" said Thyra.

"I see you have manifested a flygja; that's something even your father never managed to do. Thyra, you have allies, some you have not met yet, some you have," said Mimir. "Flygja, what is your name?"

"Helga," she answered.

"Watch out for Thyra. You are her extended eyes and ears. Watch her back. Be cautious of the creatures of Midgard."

"I will."

"To both of you . . ."

Mimir trailed off.

"What?" said Thyra.

"Quiet," he said. "We're not alone."

Thyra and Helga started to look around the peak of Mímisbrunnr.

"Hide. Now."

"What about you?" said Thyra.

"Put me back."

Thyra grabbed Mimir and placed him where they found him, then she, Helga, and Sleipnir disappeared down the side of the mountain behind the tree where they had found Mimir. They pressed against the mountain, so they remained out of view from any potential onlooker.

"What do you think it is?" whispered Helga.

Thyra shook her head.

"Mimir, my old friend, how are you?" said a mysterious voice.

"What are you doing here?"

"Is that any way to greet one of the Aesir?"

"I'm sorry. How can I help you?"

"I am beginning an endeavor, and no plan is worth implementing without consulting the wise Mimir," said the voice. "Do you have a moment?"

"For you, I have multiple," said Mimir.

The voice laughed.

"A man as smart and all-seeing—"

"Not all-seeing," said Mimir.

"I stand corrected, but a man as wise and knowing as yourself must know that a change is coming to the nine realms."

"I have sensed it."

"What do you think it is?" said the voice.

"I hate to speculate," said Mimir.

"Indulge me for one of those moments you have many of."

Mimir hesitated, then said, "I fear we may be on the cusp of Fimbulwinter."

There was a moment of silence. Thyra and Helga listened intently.

Then the voice said, "I suspected the same. Thank you for confirming. As always, your wisdom is without compare."

There was silence again. Then Mimir spoke up.

"You can come out."

Thyra and Helga emerged from their hiding.

"Who was that?" said Helga.

"Time is not on your side," said Mimir ignoring the question.

"What exactly is Fimbulwinter?" said Thyra. "I heard Gunnar speak of it, and now whoever that was."

"It's the precursor to Ragnarök. Three successive winters without an intervening summer. Damn it. You two need to go," said Mimir. "You must return to Hlíðarendi. Gunnar is not the only notable person in that town. Speak with Eir. She will help you track down the Valkyries who pursue you. You have the power within you to stop them; you just have to find them."

Thyra and Helga both noticed the shift in Mimir's mood. Whomever it was that he had just spoken to scared him.

Thyra restated Helga's question.

"Who was it you just spoke with?" she said.

"Go," said Mimir. "Now."

Hildr, Svipul, and Gunnr lingered in the air, just out of sight of Mimir, Thyra, and Helga.

"You saw who that was, right?" said Svipul.

Gunnr and Helga both nodded. Then overhead flew a black raven.

"Hugin," said Hildr.

"We have to get out of here," said Gunnr.

With that, the three Valkyries flew away from Mímisbrunnr as fast as they could.

Thyra and Helga descended Mímisbrunnr on horseback.

"I don't like all this back and forth," said Thyra. "We were just in Hlíðarendi."

"Yes, but we are much more informed now."

"The light elves are the ones who decimated Svartalfheim at the direction of Odin and Thor just to gain leverage over the Vanir," whispered Thyra.

"The Aesir are not who people thought they were. They are cruel."

"And manipulative," added Thyra.

"How do you feel?"

Thyra did not answer the question right away. She did not know.

Then she said, "Angry."

"Your parents saved lives the day the light elves attacked. It's not just the power your father possessed within you . . . it's both your parents' drive to do good. They did not have to look for Hakon's and Hillevi's families that day. They could have gone to that cave themselves and been just as fine. But they went looking for people they honestly did not seem to know that well during the most violent and chaotic moment of their lives. That is in you too."

"Is it?" said Thyra. "I left my father alone, and he was killed because of it."

"Calder was not killed because you were not there. He was killed because the people of Midgard are bigoted fools," said Helga.

"Even still . . . when you have a power like mine, even if you don't know how to control it fully . . . if you don't act, then that life you could save becomes your responsibility."

"I'm sure that is what your parents thought too. But don't blame yourself for anything that someone else does. You have the capacity for good, but you don't need to carry the weight of Midgard on your shoulders."

"That's easy for you to say. You just got here."

"And maybe it is because I just got here that I can give you a fresh perspective."

Thyra was quiet.

"Fair," she then said.

"Who do you think that was that Mimir made us hide from?"

"I heard him say Aesir," said Thyra.

"He had Mimir pretty scared, it seemed. Do you think it was Odin?"

"I don't think so. Odin used to seek the wisdom of Mimir. But after his time hanging for nine days, I don't know if he does anymore."

"Then who?"

"Your guess is as good as mine," said Thyra.

"Also, . . . Fimbulwinter . . . this all worries me. Valkyries on the run, a mysterious Aesir god asking Mimir about the end times . . . villainous light elves from the Great War," said Helga. "What is going on?"

"We should focus on what is immediately in front of us. The Valkyries are our priority. They will show up again, but it can be on our terms or theirs. I would prefer the prior."

"Agreed," said Helga.

Hildr, Svipul, and Gunnr touched down outside the hall. Svipul's tattoos were quickly fading. Gunnhild was surprised by their sudden return.

"What happened? Do you have the Bifrost?" said Gunnhild.

"Not yet," said Hildr. "Tell me, rune writer, are you proficient in the runic alphabet of other realms?"

Svipul and Gunnr looked at Hildr questionably.

Gunnhild took a second to consider Hildr's question, then said, "Yes."

"I need you to send a message to Alfheim," said Hildr.

"Wait a minute," said Gunnr, grabbing Hildr's shoulder. "What are you doing?"

"We need help," said Hildr. "You saw Odin's raven and who was at Mímisbrunnr. The whole point of this was to stay out of the path of the Aesir gods, yet we might be closer than ever to the Allfather. If we keep trying to track down Thyra ourselves, all of our efforts might be nullified."

"So, what are you suggesting?" Gunnr said.

Hildr turned away from her sister, back towards Gunnhild.

"Send a message to Alfheim, requesting Volund the Smith come to Midgard."

Gunnr forcibly turned her sister back towards her.

"Hildr, you shouldn't do this. Volund has no place amongst our ranks. He is a monster."

"You had no problem with the sacrifices necessary for our tattoos, but Volund is crossing a line?"

"We are becoming that which we were running from. We're the monsters now."

"You committed to this path the same as us," said Hildr.

"And maybe that was a mistake," said Gunnr.

"You know just as well as I do what happened to our sister," said Hildr.

"That was tragic. I know. But we cannot become the same as them," said Gunnr.

"The nine realms force you to make decisions that under lesser circumstances you may not have had to make."

"We are taking advantage of other people's plight for our own good."

"Sisters stop," said Svipul. "We should not fight amongst ourselves. There has to be a resolution to this."

"There isn't," said Gunnr and Hildr in unison.

The two stared at one another with fire in their eyes.

"Our sister Hlaðguðr was killed for no reason," said Hildr. "We are seen as nothing in the eyes of Odin. Will you fight for a god who does not even know you exist?"

"Odin didn't kill our sister Hildr," said Gunnr.

"He might as well have. He sent her to Jotunheim. She told me he had requested her to go to Jotunheim to fetch something for him that was extremely important . . . something that had been taken from him and that needed to be returned to Asgard."

"Yes, I know."

"But do you really know?" said Hildr. "Odin sent Hlaðguðr to Jotunheim to retrieve a chalice . . . it wasn't a special chalice; it wasn't valuable in any way other than Odin liked it and felt that he had been slighted by one of the giants and wanted it back. I told you Odin betrayed our sister, but what he did was even worse . . . he sent her to die for nothing."

Gunnr grabbed her sister's hand in both of hers.

"Hildr, I know what happened to Hlaðguðr was unfair. I do. But we cannot turn on the dark elves because our sister's life was wasted."

"Her life wasn't just wasted," whispered Hildr.

"What?" said Gunnr.

"Her life wasn't just wasted," she repeated.

"What do you mean?"

"I mean, it wasn't just her death that angered me. I was transporting a slain soldier to Valhalla when I overheard Hermod describing what had happened to Hlaðguðr while in Jotunheim. The giant that had stolen Odin's cup was the brother of The Builder, and just like how we feel slighted by Odin, he too felt slighted by Odin for his inability to come to Jötunheim himself, so he took his anger and frustration out on Hlaðguðr."

"Then we should be angry at the giant," said Gunnr.

"I would agree with you, but Odin knew something about Jotunheim that not many others do . . . time passes more slowly in the realm of the giants, more so than any other realm. He did not go there because one day in Asgard or Midgard or any of the other realms is equal to one year in Jotunheim. The magic that divides the realms from Asgard is a time displacement, so when the giant returned our sister, what seemed like a day later had actually been one year for her, and Hermod said she had been tortured the entire time."

The expression on Gunnr's face and Svipul's shifted.

"Why didn't you tell us that when we started down this path?" said Gunnr.

"Because I worried your conviction would shift at some point, and you'd need a strong reminder of why we are doing this."

Gunnr's eyes were red, with tears welling at their corners.

"You withheld that information to manipulate us," said Gunnr.

"You're strong, Gunnr. You're one of the fiercest warriors I have ever known. You both are. But I knew you might need a little extra motivation at some point."

"Hildr, I lied."

"About what?"

"You're not becoming a monster . . . you already are one."

She turned her back to her sister and walked over to Svipul.

"Come, sister. Let Hildr do this by herself if she wishes."

"Svipul, don't you dare follow her," said Hildr.

Gunnr turned around.

"You do this if you want. You try to summon the light elf alchemist who helped butcher thousands of dark elves so you can do the same, but we'll have no part of it."

Hildr could feel the anger within her swelling. She reached for her sword.

"You would strike me down?" said Gunnr.

Hildr let the weapon go.

"I won't stop you," said Gunnr. "But I will warn the dark elf of your intentions."

"You'll do no such thing," said Hildr, again going for her weapon.

Gunnr eyed her movements and put her hand on the hilt of her own sword.

"Sisters, stop," shouted Svipul. "What are we doing? The enemy is out there; it's not here."

"Stay out of it, Svipul," shouted Hildr. "This is between us."

"She's right, Svipul," Gunnr said. "We have to handle this now."

Svipul stepped forward, but Gunnhild touched her arm. She looked back, and Gunnhild shook her head.

Gunnr unsheathed her sword. Hildr did the same.

"They'll kill each other," whispered Svipul.

The two Valkyries charged one another. Their sword strikes were powerful and shook the leaves from the trees surrounding the hall. Gunnhild and Svipul were both forced to take a few steps back.

"I can't let them continue," said Svipul.

"This is between them," said Gunnhild. "Your intervention will not end the feelings that have been brewing."

"But if one kills the other, then what?"

"Then the issue will be settled," said Gunnhild.

Svipul looked at the rune writer in disbelief.

"You're all monsters," she said.

"You were on board with the plan before Gunnr started to question it . . . don't exclude yourself, Valkyrie."

Svipul ground her teeth. The rune writer was right.

Gunnr and Hildr's battle was the fiercest display of swordsmanship that Gunnhild had ever seen. Both would have put to shame any human warrior, no matter how skilled, but there was a clear superior between them. Gunnr was beating back Hildr.

Gunnr was relentless. Her strength was great, and her sword mastery was superior to Hildr. It was not so one-sided that Hildr stood no chance, but there is not a gambler in the nine realms who would have bet their entire fortune on Hildr less they enjoyed living on the edge. Sword strike after sword strike loosened Hildr's grip as the pain in her wrist and palm grew. She retreated to the sky, and Gunnr followed. She landed on the ground, and Gunnr met her there.

"Sister, just stop. You know you can't beat me," said Gunnr.

"If you want me to stop, you're going to have to kill me," shouted Hildr. "Because I will never stop."

Gunnr paused for a moment and looked at her sister. A deep sadness had overtaken Gunnr.

"I pity you, Hildr. You're so blinded by rage that you would do unto others the same evil we were trying to escape."

"You're just too weak to do what needs to be done."

Gunnr lifted her sword, not to deal a death blow but to knock Hildr's sword from her hands, but when she brought the weapon down, a strange and terrifying realization washed over her. Hildr blocked the strike with ease. The power dynamic had shifted, and Gunnr knew exactly why. She looked at her forearms, and the tattoos that had given her the power boost were faded, but Hildr's remained. She had gone last to get them done.

Hildr deflected Gunnr's sword strike and, without thinking, followed that deflection with a strike of her own that caught Gunnr in the abdomen. Clarity immediately came to Hildr. She released the sword and stepped backward.

"No," she whispered.

Gunnr touched her midsection at the point of entry. Blood was washing over the sword. Time seemed to slow down. Svipul and Gunnhild were running to her side as she fell to her knees.

"I'm sorry," Hildr said.

"Look at what . . . you've done," said Gunnr as blood started to seep from her lips.

"I didn't mean to."

Svipul dropped to Gunnr's side. She grabbed her sister's hand and held her as her body started to go limp.

"How could you do this?" she shouted at Hildr. "Gunnr, stay with us."

"She . . . will . . . lead you to ruin," said Gunnr with her dying breath.

Svipul embraced her sister as tears streamed down her cheeks. Gunnhild stood back from the three Valkyries, observing each.

Hildr reached for Svipul, but she swatted her hand away.

"Dry your tears," said Hildr. "We will prepare her funerary ceremony immediately."

An hour later, the two sisters placed the body of Gunnr atop a pyre.

"Lo, there do I see my father. Lo, there do I see my mother and my sisters and my brothers. Lo, there do I see the line of my people back to the beginning. Lo, there do they call to me; they bid me take my place among them in the halls of Valhalla, where thine enemies have been vanquished, where the brave shall live forever. Nor shall we mourn but rejoice for those that have died the glorious death," said Svipul.

She took the torch she was holding and lit the pyre. As the fires grew, casting an ominous glow upon Hildr and Svipul, Hildr turned to her sister.

"This changes nothing," she said. "We will mourn our sister, but we are still going to Svartalfheim."

"I know," said Svipul. "But we are not going as sisters. From now on, you are more dead to me than Gunnr and Hlaðguðr."

There was a quiet between them. The only sound was that of the wood crackling. Embers floated up into the air as the fire burned hotter, dotting the night sky with oranges and yellows.

TWENTY-ONE

EIR

Hildr pulled Gunnhild aside after the fire turned to glowing embers.

"Gunnr disagreed, and Svipul is unhappy about it, but that does not matter. I need you to send a message to Alfheim."

"Sending messages via the World Tree is not that easy. We'll need Ratatoskr to do so. Only he can carry messages between realms without a Bifrost key," said Gunnhild. "Do you know of what I speak?"

"The squirrel."

"I know the Alfheim runic alphabet, so composing a message will not be a problem. I just don't know where to find Ratatoskr."

"I do," said Svipul.

"Where is he?" Hildr said.

"Hvergelmir. He likes to taunt the dragon Níðhöggr who lives there."

"Can I ask if Ratatoskr can simply travel between the realms, why do you need the dark elf's Bifrost key?" said Gunnhild.

"Because after the Great War, the dark elves wisely used their knowledge of seidr magic to construct a shield around their realm so that only Bifrost keys given to dark elves could be used to access the realm."

"I see."

Thyra and Helga reached the base of the mountain. The entire way down, the two reflected on the conversation with Mimir.

"My parents met with him when they first arrived in Midgard. They warned him of what we are facing now. If only they could have told us what to do."

"I think seeing runes are better at providing guidance rather than a clear vision of the future. They'll give you an idea of what you need to do or what you can likely expect."

"How do you know?"

Helga threw up her hands.

"Besides, if your parents gave you all the answers, this journey would be theirs, not yours," said Helga.

Thyra laughed. "That's a rosy way of putting things."

Helga smiled.

"We do know our next step."

"We speak with Eir," said Thyra.

Svipul and Hildr took flight to hasten their journey to Hvergelmir. Hildr's tattoos were fading, and she could feel the power boost drifting away.

"The strength is fleeting for now, but once it is permanent, we will be able to defy the gods," she whispered.

"Sister, what can he do that we cannot?"

"You heard Mimir. Volund is obsessed with this power that the dark elf has. We need to track down Thyra without attracting the Aesir gods' attention. Volund can track her for us, and he'll be incentivized to do so because of who she is," said Hildr. "We get the Bifrost key from her. He gets her."

"Volund is a madman," said Svipul.

"Svipul. You know what we are planning. You know what Gunnhild will have to do to make our runes work permanently. You're either on board with what we have to do or not."

Svipul didn't respond.

Hildr continued, "Volund is undoubtedly one of the vilest creatures in the nine realms. I know this. Gunnr saw his work firsthand when she used to serve Alfheim and escorted so many of his victims to Valhalla and

Helheim. She knew him better than most. I saw his work too when he killed the dark elf's parents. He is no better than the Aesir gods . . . he is no better than me . . . but we need him now."

"Gunnr was right," whispered Svipul.

Hildr glanced back at her sister but chose not to respond.

Thyra and Helga rode through the night and arrived back in Hlíðar-endi as the sun inched its way into the sky. The gate was in full view, but Thyra knew they would not be allowed in, and she remembered that Gunnar was no longer present since he left to deal with Gissur the White, so as they neared, she steered Sleipnir off the road and into the forest that lined it.

"How do we get in?" said Helga.

"This is where you come in," said Thyra. "You look like a human. Go find Eir and bring her here."

"I think it is absurd that your presence would cause a stir."

"Thanks," said Thyra dryly.

Helga dropped down from the horse and walked up to the gate.

"Little girl," said the guard. "What are you doing out there?"

"I went for a stroll last night and lost my way."

The guard looked at her curiously.

"You should be more careful. One of our residents was recently found unconscious. We are still looking for the perpetrator."

The gate opened, and Helga entered. The guard met her on the other side.

"Were you with anyone?" he said.

"No."

The guard looked at her suspiciously.

"Who are your parents?"

Helga hesitated for a second while she thought.

"Eir," she said, gambling.

The guard's expression shifted from suspicion to apologetic.

"I'm sorry I questioned you."

He moved out of her way. Helga did not start walking right away, not believing for a moment that it had worked, but then realized if she delayed any longer, she would create unnecessary suspicion and left the guard alone. She looked back at him as he closed the door.

"Hmph," she said.

Having been instructed by Thyra to seek out Bo, she found him brewing a pot of tea.

"Can I help you, child?" he said, seeing her standing in the doorway.

Helga didn't make small talk and got straight to the point, "You know Thyra. I am here on her behalf. Can you point me in the direction of Eir?"

"Who are you?"

"My name is Helga. I am Thyra's flygja."

"You're what?"

"It doesn't matter. Can you point me in the direction of Eir?"

The teapot started to whistle, so Bo removed it from the flame. He continued to look at the girl.

"What's a flygja?"

"An extension of Thyra."

"Like a family member?"

"Not quite."

"A servant?"

"No."

"But you do her bidding?"

"Yes, but . . ."

"You're a friend of the dark elf. Come with me," he said. "I'll introduce you to Eir."

Thyra stood by Sleipnir, waiting for Helga to return. She was looking up at the sky, letting her mind wander. Her thoughts shifted to a single point.

"Why should I have to hide?" she whispered rhetorically. "Why should I have to stand out here just to prevent a fuss?"

She looked at the gate that Helga had passed through and at the guard who had returned to his post.

"What would he say if he saw me approaching?" she whispered. "Who cares?"

Thyra started to take steps towards the gate but stopped when she heard her name whispered from above. She turned around and saw Helga descending from the treetops and a winged woman alongside her.

Helga touched the ground first.

"This is Eir," she said as the Valkyrie landed beside her.

"As I am sure you've gathered, I am a Valkyrie. Helga told me about the ones who pursue you. I'm sorry this is happening," said Eir. "We are usually much more dutiful."

"Mimir sent us to find you. He said you could help us," said Thyra.

Hildr and Svipul stopped flying once Hvergelmir was within view. Resting at its peak was the dragon Níðhöggr.

"Ratatoskr makes regular appearances to agitate the dragon. We'll know he is near because his approach stirs up all of the snakes near Níðhöggr, and they descend the mountain."

"Then we wait," said Hildr.

TWENTY-TWO

A MESSAGE FOR A LIGHT ELF

"Valkyries have a tough job. We see people at their most fragile. It does not matter which realm the Valkyrie serves; all creatures face death similarly. There is a mix of fear, regret, shame, and finally, acceptance. Experiencing that daily takes its toll," said Eir. "There is also the fact that Valkyries are expected to be warriors for Odin and do his bidding. And believe me, Odin does not care about Valkyries as individuals. Now I say all that, and it still does not excuse the actions of Hildr, Gunnr, and Svipul."

"They will sacrifice what remains of my people so they can survive Ragnarök," said Thyra. "I can't let that happen. Mimir said I have the power within me to stop them, but that won't do me any good if I can't find them."

"I can help you with that," said Eir.

Eir revealed a map and opened it on a large bolder so Thyra and Helga could see it clearly.

"Valkyries have halls in the realms they serve. They are medium-sized halls. Mine is here. I will mark the halls of the three you are pursuing."

"Can I ask why you're helping us? Isn't there a code amongst the Valkyries?"

"I have a daughter with a human. I want the nine realms to be better for her, and I understand going against Odin. His ways are dangerous but so are these three Valkyries. Plus, . . . Fimbulwinter is coming, and things will only get more chaotic from here. The best I can do is help empower those fighting for the right thing."

Eir proceeded to draw x's over the locations of Hildr's, Gunnr's, and Svipul's halls.

"I want the nine realms to be better for you too. I know why you did not come to get me and instead sent Helga. What happened to the dark elves was barbaric and devastatingly tragic. It's something all Valkyries talk about to this day. And the unjustified hate directed towards you now is egregious. So, let me come with you."

Thyra hesitated momentarily and said, "Take care of your daughter. This realm needs more people like you. She needs you. I'll be fine."

"We'll . . . be fine," corrected Helga.

"The locations are a few days apart from each other. What are you going to do when you find them? Are you prepared to . . . kill them?"

"I don't know," said Thyra. "My father was adamantly against killing. But I wonder if he'd feel differently now. . . ."

"This mission they are on is life and death. They won't be playing with you. I would advise you to prepare to do what you must."

"I know."

"Are you sure you do not want company on this journey?"

"I can . . ."

"We can," said Helga.

"We can handle this," said Thyra.

"Well, know that you have allies. Know that you are not alone."

Thyra nodded. With that, Eir took flight and quickly escaped Thyra's view as she returned to the other side of the wall. Thyra looked at Helga and then the map.

"Do you trust her?" Helga said.

"I do."

"Then we better not waste any time tracking down these halls."

Hildr had been waiting for hours for Ratatoskr to appear, and patience was waning.

"How much longer?" said Hildr.

"Look," said Svipul. "The snakes are moving."

"About time."

Coming up the mountainside path en route to the dragon at the top was a larger-than-average squirrel scurrying at a galloping horse's pace.

"He can move," said Svipul.

"Let's hope he can deliver our message as quickly," said Hildr.

The two Valkyries swooped down, and before Ratatoskr could realize what happened, they grabbed him and took him into the sky.

"Let me go. Who are you? What are you doing? I swear I'm innocent."

"Quiet yourself," said Hildr. "Are you Ratatoskr?"

"Who's asking?"

"You are the squirrel who travels the World Tree," said Hildr.

"Yes. That's me. Am I dead?"

Hildr pinched his tail. He jerked at the pain.

"You felt that, didn't you?" Hildr.

"If I'm not dead, what do two Valkyries want with me?"

"We want you to deliver a message to Alfheim."

"Alfheim? You need a message sent to the light elves?"

"Can you do this?" said Svipul.

"What's in it for me?"

"You get to live," said Hildr.

Ratatoskr looked at the ground. They were currently flying above the clouds.

"That sounds fair," he said.

"Our rune writer will give you the message in the Alfheim runic alphabet. We want you to deliver it. And you're to take it directly to Volund the Smith. Do you understand?"

"Volund the Smith? You want me to take this message to the Alchemist of Alfheim."

"Is that going to be a problem?"

Ratatoskr hesitated, then remembered the Valkyries' threat.

"No, . . . he's just not someone that's usually courted."

Svipul and Hildr glanced at one another. Ratatoskr did not notice it. But if he had, he would have recognized the expression for what it was. They were saying with their eyes, "Are you sure?"

The ride was slow as Sleipnir trotted along the Midgardian road away from Hlíðarendi. The sun was high in the sky, but it was still so cold.

Helga sat behind Thyra, holding her around her waist, partly for stability and warmth.

"I can't imagine a Midgard colder than this," said Thyra. "Three consecutive winters."

"Snow from all directions. No intervening summer. And then war. The nine realms still feel the impacts of the last Great War 200 years ago."

"Ragnarök is the end of all things."

There was a silence between the two as they both contemplated what was coming. Then Helga spoke up.

"Which hall are we heading to first?"

"Gunnr's is the nearest to our current location, so we'll go there."

Helga and Thyra continued their journey on horseback, appreciating the silence of the lonely road they traveled. Water from unknown water crashed into a pond from just out of eyesight. The few birds that existed despite the cold, chirped.

"Midgard has a certain appeal. If one can get around all the other . . . nonsense," whispered Thyra.

Helga's stomach growled.

"Are you hungry?" Thyra said.

"I didn't know I needed to eat."

"What you know and don't know is bewildering."

"I'm just as perplexed by what I am as you. Trust me."

"As soon as we come across an inn, we'll stop. I am sorry I did not realize. Dark elves can go days without sustenance. Slower metabolism."

"That must be convenient for journeys like this."

"It would be, but seeing as this is my first journey, I wouldn't know."

"The first of many, I'm sure."

It was not long until Thyra and Helga came across an inn. A few horses were tied to the post outside, meaning there were people inside. Thyra and Helga cautiously approached.

"We don't have to stop if you don't want to," said Helga.

"No. We're stopping. I'm hungry too."

"But I thought . . ."

"I'm hungry too."

Thyra steered Sleipnir to the end of the post, hopped down, and hitched the horse. She walked ahead of Helga into the inn, where a few folks dined on the first floor. The chatter stopped immediately as their eyes shifted towards her. The inn's owner rushed over to the front desk where the ledger was situated.

"What . . . are you . . . doing here?" said the inn's owner, her voice shaking.

"We are hungry," said Thyra.

"I uhm . . . I . . ."

"What's the problem?" Thyra said, anger slipping into her tone.

"We just . . ."

The innkeeper looked around the room for someone to help her or back her up.

"My friend and I are looking for food."

"I understand."

"Is this not an inn? Are those people there not eating?" said Thyra.

The woman looked to her right.

"I'm sorry. But . . . just please go. We don't want any problems with a dark elf."

"I came here looking for a meal, and you are creating a problem. We're hungry. You have food."

Thyra nodded for Helga to follow her. She moved into the dining room where a few patrons were cautiously watching the dark elf and the small girl. Helga looked at the inn's owner with disappointment on her face. The woman stood in silence.

Thyra took a seat at an empty table. The nearby diners stared quietly. One of the waiters observed Thyra, but the innkeeper shook her head at her.

"We can go," whispered Helga.

"No. You're hungry. I'm hungry."

The innkeeper approached the table.

"Please leave," she said, her voice shaking.

"What is the problem? Isn't this an establishment with food? You could have already brought us a meal at this point, and we'd be on our way."

The waitress, who was instructed not to approach, waved the innkeeper to her.

"Wouldn't it be easier just to serve them?" she whispered.

"Dark elves are dangerous. It's better they just go," the innkeeper responded.

Helga leaned in and whispered as softly as she could, "It's not worth it, Thyra. Let's just leave. This isn't right, but it's just how it is."

"I waited outside the gate for you to go get Eir. I'm tired of letting their fear dictate my actions," she whispered back.

"Think of Svartalfheim. We are on a mission."

There was a pause. Then Thyra slammed her fist on the table. Everyone in the room jumped.

"All of you are pathetic," said Helga.

Thyra's eyes were glowing red.

"She means to kill us," said one of the patrons. "Look at her eyes."

Thyra stood up, and the room collectively gasped. She proceeded to exit the inn.

"Grow up," said Helga to the innkeeper before following Thyra outside.

Thyra was standing by Sleipnir.

"Are you ok?" said Helga.

Thyra turned to face her. Her eyes were red still, but not because of her power.

"They're small, minded people," assured Helga. "Unwilling to see you for who you truly are."

"I don't need them to see me for who I am. I just don't want to be seen as a monster."

"I know."

Helga extended a hand and placed it on Thyra's arm.

"Humans are afraid because they're weak. In many ways, they're like the Valkyries we face. Scared, hypocritical, and violent."

"Let's find you something to eat," Thyra said.

"It's ok. I found something," said Helga holding up some bread she swiped from a table.

Thyra smiled.

"Fools," said Helga.

Hildr and Svipul dropped Ratatoskr at the feet of Gunnhild.

"Have you prepared the message?" said Hildr.

Gunnhild picked up a small scroll from the table to her left. Hildr gestured for her to hand it over, which she did. Though she could not fully understand the Alfheim runic alphabet, it overlapped enough with the Midgardian runic alphabet, and she understood the gist of the message.

"Carry this to Volund, and do not delay," she said to Ratatoskr before strapping it to his back with twine.

"Yes, mam," said the squirrel.

"Come back here once the message has been delivered with proof you delivered the message if Volund is to refuse our request for whatever reason."

"Understood."

"If you do not come back and he does not come, we'll assume you betrayed us and . . ."

"I know. I'm a dead squirrel."

"Good. Now get."

Ratatoskr ran off, and as soon as he was out of sight, a flash of rainbow signified his journey between the realms.

TWENTY-THREE

THE ALCHEMIST OF ALFHEIM

Alfheim was not a realm Ratatoskr often visited. It was too bright. No shadows anywhere. It was nauseating and unsettling. Being small, he preferred shadows—they let him escape when necessary. But not in Alfheim. He always had to be too cautious. And this time, he had to be especially careful since he was going to meet with quite possibly the most dangerous light elf of all time.

"How did I get caught up in this?" he whispered as he scampered along the paved roads.

Ahead of him was his destination. It was a large hall near a flowing stream at the edge of town. He knew of Volund's hall from the stories the Eagle would tell him from his own journeys across the realms. He would tell Ratatoskr of all the places he should visit, but he always warned him to stay clear of Volund's hall—but what choice did he have this time?

A few light elves noticed Ratatoskr running along the street, but they paid him no mind. He ignored them too. Soon he exited the town proper and entered a vast field with grass hardly much taller than him. It was noticeably warmer in Alfheim than in Midgard. On the other side of the field was Volund's hall. Ratatoskr felt the anxiety of meeting Volund sweep through his little body. He stopped.

"How could they find me?" he said. "I don't want any part in this."

He pulled at the twine wrapped around his midsection. It slowly started to loosen.

But before the note dropped, he said, "Do I really want two angry Valkyries hunting me for the rest of my days? I've heard their grudges can be legendary."

He looked up at the bright blue-almost-white sky.

"No. Let me just get this done and get out of here."

He exited the field. Volund's hall was now directly in front of him, and up close, it was not quite as big as it seemed from afar. Maybe that was a sign; there was not as much to fear as he thought. The Eagle tended to exaggerate, and who knows what happened during the Great War anyway?

Ratatoskr made his way to the entrance of the hall. Just as he was trying to figure out how to open the door, it opened on its own. The darkness inside the hall starkly contrasted with the overabundance of light outside. Just as the smaller size of the hall helped to ease Ratatoskr's fear, this darkness sent his anxiety through the roof.

He eyed the entrance cautiously and slowly poked his head in the door.

"Hello," he said. "Is anyone here."

"Come in," said a bodiless voice.

Ratatoskr inched his little body through the doorway but stopped.

"Nope. This does not feel right," he said and turned around. "If I have to spend the rest of my days evading those Valkyries, then so be it."

But just as Ratatoskr was about to leave, he felt a small tug on his tail. He did not hesitate to teleport away from this realm, but his gift was not working.

"Ratatoskr," said that same ominous, bodiless voice. "Leaving so soon?"

He felt the tug on his tail increase in strength, and then he was whisked away into the darkness, and the door shut behind him.

Thyra and Helga left that miserable inn, but the people that shunned Thyra still made appearances in her mind. She tried pretending she did not care, but she did.

"If we are going to face those Valkyries, you're probably going to want to know how to use this power inside of you," said Helga.

"You're right," Thyra said. "I was focused on finding them . . . what happens when we do?"

"Let's practice controlling it. There is a clearing behind those trees. We can stop there."

Moments later, Thyra hitched Sleipnir to a tree and moved to the center of the clearing.

"What happened the first time you used your power?" said Helga.

"I was angry. I was . . . sad. They had just killed my father."

Saying it aloud took her right back to that moment, and Thyra's eyes glowed red.

"Is anger what triggers it?"

"I don't know."

"Whatever you're feeling now, try holding onto it," said Helga.

Thyra concentrated and could feel the energy coursing through her, but in no way could she control it, and as quickly as she felt it, it faded away, and her eyes stopped glowing.

"I had it," said Thyra. "But it was fleeting."

"At least you know you can tap into at will. Try again."

Thyra tilted her palms skyward and focused on manifesting this power in her hands. Her fingertips grew warmer, but as quick as it came, it went.

"It could be a defense mechanism," said Helga as she picked up a small rock.

"What are you doing?"

"Just bear with me."

"Stop."

Helga chucked the rock at Thyra. Thyra deflected it with her right hand, and the rock exploded. Her hand was glowing red.

Astonishment washed over both their faces. Helga picked up another rock and tossed it. Thyra deflected that one too.

"That worked," said Helga.

"So, it is a defense mechanism?"

"At least for now. You just need to tap into whatever it is that triggers when you're being attacked and master it."

"Is that all?" Thyra said sarcastically.

"I know. Easier said than done."

"Much easier said than done."

"But if anyone can do it, you can."

"I appreciate your enthusiasm," said Thyra.

"Try projecting your power. See the tree ahead of you. Try and hit it."

Thyra raised her hands, palms facing away from her. Her fingertips warmed like before, but that was it. She concentrated as best she could but nothing.

"That's ok. We can keep working on that," said Helga.

"I'll get it in time."

"Preferably before we face Hildr, Gunnr, and Svipul."

Thyra laughed.

"Preferably."

Svipul spied Hildr staring at the expanse of Midgard visible from the hilltop where they made home base. She watched her sister, standing there with her hands clasped behind her back, stoic, lost in thought. She had never seen Hildr so contemplative. Svipul considered going to her sister but opted against it. Instead, she went inside the hall, where she found Gunnhild reading.

"Tell me, how does a human become so proficient in the art of rune writing?" she said.

Gunnhild looked up at the Valkyrie.

"Years and years of training . . . and an excellent mentor."

"Long ago, manipulating runes and seidr magic was mostly lost on humans."

"I'm aware."

"And now, some of you are the most skilled practitioners in the nine realms."

"I wouldn't say that," said Gunnhild, appreciating the comment and feigning modesty.

"It's true. Surely there are some better, but not many. And it's interesting because seidr magic comes more naturally to elves."

"Just because something comes more naturally to someone does not mean they will be the most skilled at it. Sometimes what matters is hard work and dedication."

"Hard work and dedication. That was Gunnr. She was strong. Skilled. Someone I really looked up to."

"Can I ask you something?" said Gunnhild.

"What?"

"Why are you doing this? You're clearly conflicted. Gunnr turned on Hildr. I will do what you want as long as I get to see my husband again. But it doesn't seem to me that you're clear on what you want."

Svipul hesitated to respond, but said, "You said I'm a monster. I don't want to be one, though, and I am afraid I don't know how to stop Hildr."

"And talking to her clearly won't help, considering what happened to Gunnr."

"I know we have gone too far."

"You could run."

"To where? Even if I got away from her, I'd still have to contend with Odin and his recklessness. Besides, I would still be complicit in whatever Hildr and Volund do. You are lucky human . . . you aren't bound by some destiny that compels you to take part in a foolish war. The Norns have spared your species from that kind of doomed fate."

"Svipul. The Norns don't control the fates of any species. They use the past to interpret the future. I know because I have met with them."

"You've consulted the Norns?"

"Long ago, with my master. Her master instructed her to take me there. That was when they told me . . . told us how they work."

"What? What are you saying?"

"I'm saying your fate is fluid. Everyone's fate is," said Gunnhild.

"I . . . this can't be . . . you're lying."

"Why would I lie? I gain nothing by telling you this."

"You're trying to manipulate me."

"I want to see my husband again. I need you and your sister to release me. So maybe you're right—I would tell you what you want to hear to free me, but I'm not lying. The Norns do not write your fate, but they will tell you what you need to hear just as I am now telling you."

"You're not lying. I can tell. Human hearts beat faster when they're lying."

"I felt just as confused when I heard it too."

"Gunnr didn't have to die."

Svipul turned around.

"What are you about to do?" said Gunnhild.

"What I should have done a long time ago."

She started for the hall door, but as she approached, she saw the flashes of a bright rainbow and the thunderous clap of a Bifrost bridge touching the ground. Then standing at the door was Hildr.

"He's here." She said.

Thyra deflected rock after rock with increasing mastery over her power. But she could not project the red energy her body generated, nor will it into existence when not directly attacked.

"I have an idea," said Helga.

"I'm listening."

"Let's try using your gift as a projectile one more time, but this time visualize that tree as the innkeeper or better yet . . . as the woman who first killed Calder."

Immediately, Thyra's thoughts shifted to her finding her father dead; just like that, her eyes turned glowing red.

"That's it," said Helga.

She raised her palm towards the tree, and a blast of energy exploded forth and fragmented the tree into tiny pieces. As quickly as the power presented itself, it disappeared.

"You did it," shouted Helga.

Thyra took stock of the debris scattered about the area.

"I did."

Hildr led Svipul and Gunnhild out of the hall. The three women were itching with anticipation.

Standing near the cliff was a man dressed in all white. A Bifrost key was in his hand, and a spear strapped to his back. He looked at the two

Valkyries and the human approaching and smiled. His expression was sinister. His eyes were cold and did not match the joy his mouth was trying to convey.

"Welcome, Volund," said Hildr.

"It's been a long time since I journeyed to Midgard," he said.

"We appreciate you coming."

"I received your message. How could I pass up tracking down the daughter of Hagen and Ase? Where is she now."

"Mimir sent her to Hlíðarendi."

"To meet with Eir, no doubt," said Volund. "She'll likely tell the girl what to do next. She may even tell her where you can be found."

"Is she going to come for us?" said Svipul.

"She might," said Volund. "Her parents were a cautious pair who may have had a warning for her of your arrival. I know they had a seeing rune."

"They did warn her . . . through Mimir," said Hildr.

"Then I would say yes; Eir probably instructed her where to find you. Her parents cared for the wellbeing of Svartalfheim, and if they used the seeing rune and saw you, then one can assume they would try to stop you."

"They did not want us to get the Bifrost key," Said Hildr. "They wouldn't put their daughter in harm's way."

"Then she is acting of her own volition. But either way, she is likely looking for you."

"Then we don't need you," said Svipul. "We can let her come to us."

Hildr threw a sharp glance at her sister.

"Volund is our guest," she said sternly.

Volund raised his hand, holding the Bifrost key.

"It's ok," he said softly. "I would give you my key, but I understand Svartalfheim is protected. I'll find this dark elf and make sure you get hers. It is the least I can do for alerting me to her whereabouts."

A rainbow crashed in front of him, and when it was gone, a massive eagle with a saddle on its back was perched. Five light elves dressed in black and white robes on horseback also appeared.

"My own creations," said Volund with a sinister smile.

He mounted the massive eagle.

"We will split up and visit the halls of these two Valkyries and their sister Gunnr," said Volund to his men. "You know their locations. We're looking for the dark elf daughter of Hagen and Ase."

"Volund before you go . . . where is Ratatoskr? He was supposed to come back here after delivering the message," said Svipul.

"The squirrel . . . a creature that can travel the realms without a Bifrost, has always fascinated me. I kept him. I'll uncover how his powers work just like I will the dark elf's."

With that, the giant eagle flapped its mighty wings, and Volund took to the sky. The light elves on horseback departed in different directions.

Svipul and Hildr looked at one another.

"Remind me again why we need Volund?" said Svipul.

"We need to keep Odin off of our trail. Besides, the more time she spends on the road, the more time she has to master her powers. The nature of her power is unknown, but if that outburst earlier is any indicator of what she is capable of, then I'm not rushing into that bout without our tattoos."

"But can we chance working with him?" said Svipul looking up at the fading silhouette of the giant eagle and the man atop it. "Why do they already know the locations of our halls?"

TWENTY-FOUR

FIRST ENCOUNTER

The sun was setting on Thyra and Helga as they neared the first hall on the map given to them by Eir. They slowed their approach to a trot.

"We should go on foot from here," said Thyra.

Helga nodded and levitated off the back of the horse. Thyra hopped down as well and hitched Sleipnir to a tree. She put her index finger to her lips.

"We'll be right back," Thyra whispered.

Helga and Thyra left the horse and made for the hall, which they could see just beyond a few trees.

"What if we find them?" said Helga.

"I don't know."

"We should have trained more."

Thyra made a fist. She tried manifesting her powers, but nothing happened.

"I'll be honest with you. I'm extremely nervous right now," said Helga.

"I am too. It's ok."

"We aren't ready."

"Helga, it's ok. You stay here, and I'll go."

"No. I'm coming. I'm just . . ."

"I'm scared too."

"I'm not just afraid for us—what do you do if you—well, if you have to . . ."

"Kill?"

Helga nodded.

"I don't know that either," said Thyra. "I'm hoping I can just be extremely persuasive."

"They're running from Odin. I don't think they're going to run from you."

The two reached the tree line and knelt behind some bushes. They observed the hall and its surroundings. There did not appear to be anyone home.

"It's getting dark, and there aren't any torches burning," whispered Helga.

"I'll get a closer look."

Before Helga could protest that decision, Thyra was already moving away from the tree line. She crept into the opening and scurried to the side of the hall. She pressed her back against the wall and inched towards the nearest window.

"Be careful," whispered Helga.

Thyra listened intently as she got closer to the window. She did not hear anything. She peeked inside and saw no one. She looked back at Helga and shrugged her shoulders.

"No one is home," she said.

Helga stood up and ran over.

"The hall is empty?" she said.

"Yes."

Helga peaked through the window also.

"Do we keep going then? To the next hall?" said Helga.

"No. Let's look for clues."

"Clues to what?"

"To why the Valkyries are on this mission in the first place."

"We know."

"Beyond the blood, I mean. What is motivating them?"

"Does it matter?"

"It does to me. It is my people they're after. I want to know at least why."

"All right."

Thyra observed Helga scurry around to the front of the hall. She then followed. The two pressed on the doors and entered. It was immediately evident that no one had been home in quite some time. A layer of dust covered everything.

"Strange," said Thyra.

"What?"

Thyra ran her finger through a layer of dust that covered a table next to her.

"They've been on this course of action for a long time," she said, wiping the dust from her finger on her pelt.

"Take a look at this," said Helga after picking up and reading over a scroll.

She handed it to Thyra. She read it.

"There was a fourth sister," said Thyra.

"It says Odin sent her on a mission from which she did not make it home."

"So, are they trying to get back at Odin?"

"Or just survive."

"By killing dark elves."

Helga shrugged.

Thyra put the scroll down on the table by her side.

"There are so few of us left, and a blow like this would be detrimental."

"It definitely wouldn't help."

"This isn't funny."

"Thyra, you need to start thinking seriously about what you are prepared to do when the time comes," said Helga.

"I know."

"These sisters will not hesitate to kill you . . . and me to get what they want."

"I know, Helga."

"I think you must also be prepared to do what you must."

Thyra's attention shifted from Helga to something outside the hall.

"What?" said Helga noticing the change in demeanor.

"We aren't alone," she whispered.

The two took cover behind the table as the hall doors opened.

"So, this is a Valkyrie hall," said a man dressed in a black and white robe.

"Who is he?" whispered Helga.

Thyra shook her head.

The doors closed behind him as he slowly walked through the hall. The hood of his robe covered most of his face. A sword hung by his side. He would soon be upon them.

"What are we going to do?" whispered Helga.

"Let's see what he wants."

"No."

Thyra stood up despite Helga's protest. The man looked her way.

"There you are," he said.

"Who are you, and what are you doing here?" said Thyra, placing her hand on the hilt of Gambanteinn.

"Who I am is not important, but I can tell you that I've been sent to find you—Thyra."

Thyra tightened her grip.

"Where is the rest of the Bifrost key in your possession?" said the man.

Helga started to rise, but Thyra gestured for her to remain hidden.

"I don't know what you're talking about."

"Don't play dumb. We both know you have it."

"Honestly. I don't know what you're talking about. I have never even seen a Bifrost key."

The man sighed and looked down.

"One last chance—are you going to produce the key, or am I going to have to take it?" said the man.

Thyra unsheathed her sword.

"Not wise," He whispered.

"I know how to use it."

The man leaped into the air, drawing his blade as he did. He was fast. Faster than Thyra expected. He brought his sword down where she was standing. She deflected, but he was strong. Stronger than she expected. The clash reverberated up through her arm. The man jumped backward and quickly prepared for another strike.

He shot forward a second time. Thyra had a better idea of what to expect and adjusted her stance accordingly. She defended, but the force with which their two swords clashed pushed her back a few inches. The man followed up with a third swipe of his blade, and Thyra retreated away from it. She left a trail of cleared dust on the floor.

From the corner of his eye, the man noticed Helga. "Who are you?" he said.

"Get out of here. I can handle this," Thyra shouted at Helga while keeping her attention on the aggressor.

Thyra went on the offensive, attempting to break the man's attention away from Helga. However, the mysterious foe effectively defended each and parried the last one, forcing Thyra to defend.

"You may be a special girl, but you're no sword fighter, and I was born for this," said the man.

He removed his hood and disrobed, revealing a sleek armor and that he was . . .

"You're a light elf," said Thyra noticing his pointed ears.

"I am," he said, grinning.

"Are you Volund?" said Thyra.

He laughed.

"Odin, no . . . just a humble servant."

The man brought his sword to the ready.

"You're going to give me the missing piece of the Bifrost key, or I'll kill her after defeating you, and don't fool yourself into thinking this is a fight you can win."

Thyra glanced at Helga. She clenched her left hand into a fist, trying to manifest her powers, but only her fingers were warming.

"What's it going to be?" said the man.

She looked back his way.

"Helga, run."

Thyra lunged for the light elf. As her sword clanged against his, Helga sprung to her feet.

Despite Thyra's best attempt, the light elf quickly put her back on the defensive, but unbeknownst to her, she was glowing red. He swung, Thyra blocked, but the force was enough to send her flying. She smashed against the wall at the end of the hall, and the power building up within her exploded. Part of the hall crumbled. Debris was everywhere. A smoke plume rose through the collapsed roof.

The light elf was breathing heavily. Had he been any closer, he'd be a goner. He quickly grabbed Helga by the collar and put the sword to her neck.

"Enough girl," he shouted. "Give me the piece of the Bifrost key now."

Thyra picked herself up; rubble slid off her and crashed to the ground. Dust and floating pieces of debris were settling all around her.

"Let her go," she said.

"First, the key."

He pressed the blade to Helga's neck. A line of blood seeped onto her collar. Thyra tried manifesting her powers again, but just like usual, only her fingers started to warm.

"The key," shouted the light elf.

"I can't," shouted Thyra.

The light elf pressed the blade even deeper into Helga's neck, and the line of blood grew.

Thyra let out a deep sigh, reached into the pouch she kept on her person, and produced the missing piece of the Bifrost key.

"Place it on the ground and back away from it."

She did as instructed.

"Thyra don't. Think about Svartalfheim," shouted Helga.

"Be quiet," said the light elf before hitting her on the head.

The force with which he hit her rattled Helga, but the blow triggered something within her. With one mighty swing of her fist, she slammed the light elf in the crotch. Helga hit the armor, but the might packed into her tiny fist crumbled the armor. The light elf's eyes bulged as he gasped for air. He dropped the sword and doubled over, slowly backing away from Helga and Thyra.

"What . . . was . . . that?" he said between gasps.

"You're strong?" said Thyra.

Helga picked up the light elf's sword, turned around, and pointed the blade in his direction.

"It's over," she said.

Thyra grabbed the piece of the Bifrost key and put it back in her pouch, then moved forward to stand next to Helga. The light elf was still trying to catch his breath when Thyra put her hand on his shoulder and forced him to the ground.

"Take a seat."

His face was red. Tears were streaming down his cheeks. His breathing was normalizing, but he would not be right for a long time.

"How did you know where we were?" said Thyra.

"I . . . I didn't," he said. "We were . . . all . . . sent to . . . the different halls."

"We?" said Helga.

"The . . . others. The other . . . light elves."

"You all serve Volund?" said Thyra.

The light elf nodded. Thyra and Helga glanced at each other.

"Does Volund serve the Valkyries?"

The light elf shook his head.

"Then why are you doing their bidding?"

"The Valkyries . . . get the . . . key," said the light elf. "Volund gets . . . you."

Thyra sighed.

"Why are you so strong?" said Thyra.

"Enhanced . . . his doing. Please. I need help."

"You'll live," said Thyra.

The light elf fell to his side in the fetal position.

"What are we going to do if Volund is looking for you?" said Helga.

Thyra breathed deeply through her nose and let out a deep sigh.

"This does change things," she said. "The Valkyries were bad enough, but Volund, . . . he helped slaughter my people. He killed my parents.

And clearly, he's mastered something that boosts abilities. Who knows what he's done for himself?"

"We can devise a new plan," said Helga.

"We're going to have to," said Thyra.

The light elf on the ground started crying.

"I will never have kids," he moaned.

"What do we do with him?" Helga said.

Moments later

"You can't leave me like this," said the light elf, hogtied in chains scoured from the hall's cellar.

"If you keep screaming, we'll gag you too," said Helga.

The light elf grew quiet.

"Get his sword," said Thyra.

Helga strapped it to her waist.

"We have a few questions for you," Thyra said. "The first being—how many of you are there?"

"Five."

"And that includes Volund?"

"No. Five plus Volund."

"Are you all strong?" said Thyra.

"Yes."

"Can Volund be reasoned with?"

This question did not solicit an answer but rather a laugh.

"Fool, this man cannot be reasoned with. He cannot be bargained with. He has no pity, remorse, or fear and he is coming for you."

"What does he want?"

"That power inside of you."

"Where he is."

"I don't know, but more importantly, it doesn't matter. He'll find you, and when he does . . . ask if he can do his experiments on your corpse."

"Shut your mouth," shouted Helga.

"It's fine," said Thyra. "He's just trying to scare me."

"Well, he's scaring me."

"You would be wise to be afraid. There has never been anything or anyone like Volund. He's gone beyond the nine realms to learn a magic foreign to our realms."

"Alchemy," said Thyra.

"What is it?"

"I don't know. Honest."

"Where does it come from then? What is this place beyond our realms?"

"I don't know that either."

Thyra and Helga looked at one another and, without saying a word, decided he was telling the truth.

"When this is all over, we'll set you free," said Thyra. "Until then, drink that water next to you slowly."

"Wait a minute. You can't leave me here like this."

"Would you rather I kill you?" said Thyra.

The light elf was quiet.

"Light elves have slow metabolisms like dark elves, right?" said Helga as they returned to Sleipnir.

"Of course," said Thyra. "I think so."

T W E N T Y - F I V E

A HALL TO CALL
YOUR OWN

Svipul sat with Gunnhild in the hall. She watched the woman study her runes.

"I'm afraid," said Svipul breaking the silence between the two.

Gunnhild looked up from her runes.

"What of?" she said.

"That we have made a mistake."

"What mistake would that be?" said Gunnhild putting the runes away in a small pouch.

Svipul looked through one of the windows of the hall at her sister, who had not left her place by the cliff. With her hands clasped behind her back like usual, she stared off into the distance.

"Gunnr is dead. Hlaðguðr is dead. Hildr is dead to me. I am alone, and for what reason?"

"Svipul, it sounds like you should talk with your sister about your concerns."

Svipul looked at Gunnhild for what felt like an eternity, then proceeded to get up and exit the hall.

"These Valkyries," whispered Gunnhild. "They better honor their end of the bargain."

Svipul cautiously approached her sister. Hildr looked from the corner of her eyes as she approached.

"What?" she said.

"Volund has been gone for a little while. How confident are you in him?"

"Very."

Svipul reached out and touched Hildr on the shoulder.

"Look at me," she said.

Hildr turned to face her sister. The cool winter air washed over them.

"How confident are you? Truthfully."

Hildr was quiet.

"Your silence says it all," said Svipul.

Hildr pinched her nose and then ran her fingers through her hair.

"What are we doing?" Svipul said. "Is this worth it?"

"We're in too deep now," said Hildr.

"No, we aren't. He is just a light elf. We are Valkyries. We don't need him."

"You don't know what you're talking about."

"What?"

"He might be a light elf, but he is one of the most twisted and greatest minds of the nine realms. He is the reason Thor suggested sending the light elves after the dark elves. He has the ear of the Aesir. And that's because they respect his cruelty and brilliance."

"Why then did you suggest summoning him here?"

"We were desperate."

"We are even more so now."

"You don't know that. This could work."

"What did Gunnr know?"

"What?"

"She knew how bad this man is. What did she know?"

Hildr hesitated.

"Tell me."

"Volund played more of a role later in the war after the slaughter of the dark elves. The Aesir had a hall in Alfheim where they kept Vanir prisoners. So, impressed by his actions in Svartalfheim, they put Volund in charge of it, and with his tendency to experiment and a near endless supply of low-level Vanir gods to toy with, some of the true horrors of the Great War were realized."

"Gunnr was a Valkyrie in Alfheim back then."

"So, she saw it all. His work showed no consideration for health, safety, . . . suffering. He wanted to know what made the Vanir, Vanir. His interest was in behavior, culture, the body, and societies, but his methods were cruel. His victims were dismembered, some were intentionally infected with disease, and others were sterilized. The things Gunnr saw kept her up at night, and this is Gunnr we're talking about . . . a ruthless warrior in her own right."

"This is the man we have brought to Midgard . . . that we have partnered with?" Svipul shouted. "A sadist friend of the Aesir."

"I never said a friend. Volund has no real loyalties . . . he works with his own interests in mind, and for the time being, our interests are aligned."

"Then I repeat my question from earlier . . . why do his men know where all the Valkyrie halls are?" said Svipul.

Thyra and Helga rode in silence for a while after leaving the first of the Valkyrie halls. The sun was setting, and in the darkness, the cold was piercing.

"You did quite well back there," said Thyra.

"I don't know what came over me. All I knew was I didn't want to die there."

"Helga, I want you to know I'm glad you're with me. I don't know if I could make this journey by myself."

"I'm glad to be with you too, but know that you are stronger than you give yourself credit for."

The two continued in silence for a while longer. The hooves of Sleipnir and the creatures of the forest lining the road were the only audible sounds. Thyra and Helga were in the part of Midgard furthest from any town, and it was oddly peaceful. But they remained vigilant. The creatures of Midgard could be quite ferocious.

"The next hall is not far. We should be there in just a few hours," said Helga.

"And that means more of Volund's men."

"It also means potentially the Valkyries."

"Sooner or later, you are going to have to face them. Valkyries are powerful creatures. They usher the dead or dying to the afterlife and serve as the warriors of the gods, but their power is dependent on their connection to the World Tree, and because of that, they will never be as powerful as you can be. Your power comes from within."

Hildr and Svipul approached Gunnhild in the hall. Gunnhild had not returned to tinkering with her runes, for she anticipated a conversation with the two remaining Valkyries. She watched them approach and take a seat on either side of her.

"We need to discuss Volund and how we move forward," said Hildr.

"I suspected you might," Gunnhild said.

"Bringing him here was not the wisest decision made recently," added Svipul.

"Mistakes are made during war," Gunnhild said.

"We are not at war," Svipul said.

"Yet," said Hildr.

"I have a suggestion," said Gunnhild.

"What is it?" Hildr said.

"Once you're all-powerful, it may be wise to find a hall that befits your new strength. A place to call your own, divorced from your anchor realm. This will be a place you choose to live, rather than one you are forced to serve from."

"What are you suggesting?" Said Hildr.

"Volund can't be trusted. We all know that. Gunnr knew it most of all. But before he betrays you, you can strike first."

"Are you suggesting we take his hall?" said Hildr.

Gunnhild nodded.

"It's his hall from the Great War, so its defenses are strong, but you will have a Bifrost key and be physically superior."

"Physically sure," said Svipul. "But Volund is a tinkerer and will surely have weapons at his disposal we aren't privy to."

"If you can't handle a single light elf no matter how much of a tinkerer, then all of your efforts to survive Ragnarök are for naught because that'll be worse than anything Volund will throw at you," said Gunnhild.

"She has a point," said Hildr. "Volund would be a proper test of what we can do, and his hall is a prize worth taking."

"Gunnhild, what do you get out of this?" said Svipul.

"You took me from my husband, and it is he whom I want to return to, but I was a rune writer before I was a wife, and the trinkets hidden away in Volund's hall are items I can only dream of. If you breach it, I could be the greatest rune writer of all time."

"Humans," laughed Hildr. "Your kind might be fragile, but you are clever and deviant."

"Volund's men are slaves. We need only turn one of them to our side."

TWENTY-SIX

THE STORY OF FENRIR AND GLEIPNIR

Thyra and Helga stopped to make camp. The fire was warm and provided much needed light in the dense forest at the edge of known Midgardian territory. Thyra had tied Sleipnir to a nearby tree.

Thyra waved her hands over the fire. The warmth she felt differed from the heat she generated when she tried to manifest her powers. It was external, whereas the power she created was internal and radiated outward.

Helga sat across from her staring at the flames. She looked lost in thought. Thyra wondered how far she had strayed from her original mind that was born of her own. Helga had said she was her own person. Would she want to go her own way? Would she grow up? These were questions Thyra was not sure she would be able to get an answer to until they either happened or did not.

The glow of the fire danced on the trees that surrounded them. The full moon was partially visible through the dense canopy.

"Do you know any stories?" Helga said.

"What kind of stories?"

"Anything. Something to pass the time."

"There was one my father told me a long time ago. It's a common misconception to be attested to the dwarves, but the dark elves did it."

"Let's hear it," said Helga.

"The story begins with the trickster god Loki. He had three children with the giant Angrboda. Most people know the first child . . . the World Serpent Jörmungandr. The second child is the Goddess Hel of Helheim. But few know of the third child . . . the powerful wolf, so fewer know of his binding."

"I'm intrigued."

"You should be," laughed Thyra. "As the story was told to me, the Aesir had many concerns regarding the three children. The gods had premonitions that they would bring an end to the Aesir. Obviously, that has yet to happen. But their concerns were that Hel would not release Baldr from Helheim and that Jörmungandr would kill Thor. But the biggest concern was that Fenrir would devour Odin."

"Fenrir is the wolf?"

"Fenrir is the wolf. To keep these concerns from becoming a reality, the Aesir threw Jörmungandr into the sea and Hel they banished to Helheim. I should add that their concern about Hel they seemed to have inadvertently created. But Fenrir was such a problem that they did not want to let him out of their sight. So, they raised the wolf themselves in Asgard, and only Tyr, the god of war, was brave enough to feed the beast. As the story goes, Fenrir grew so fast that he started to alarm the Aesir, and they decided he would not get to stay in Asgard freely, so they devised a plan to bind him. The Aesir tricked Fenrir into letting them bind him to test his strength. They tried many different chains, and each time Fenrir would break free."

"What did the Aesir do?"

"Eventually, they became so frustrated that they sent a messenger to Svartalfheim . . . keep in mind this is long before the Great War . . . and requested a chain be forged. Now, this is usually where those who do know this story confuse things . . . they always think that it was the dwarves who forged this chain. While the dwarves are the most skilled blacksmiths in the nine realms, the Aesir wanted a chain forged by those with mastery of seidr magic *and* the ability to forge, and the only beings that fit that description were the dark elves. Light elves were skilled practitioners of seidr magic but were not known for the forgery, and dwarves were fine forgers but were not known for their seidr magic. So, a few dark elves, whose names have been lost to time, got together and forged a chain made of impossible ingredients."

"What ingredients?" said Helga.

"A cat's footsteps, the beard of a woman, the roots of mountains, the breath of a fish, and the spittle of a bird . . . things that do not exist, thus making the chain they forged impossible to break. They called this chain Gleipnir. The Aesir presented Gleipnir to Fenrir, but for the first time, the wolf suspected he was being tricked and refused to be bound by the new chain. But the gods insisted it was not a trick. Fenrir told them that if one of the gods would put their hand in his jaws, he would accept being bound. None of the gods agreed because they knew they were lying and that whoever did it would lose their hand. But the only god who had been brave enough to feed Fenrir was the only god brave enough to put his hand in his jaws. The other gods bound Fenrir in Gleipnir, and when he realized he could not break free, he bit Tyr's hand clean off and swallowed it. Shortly after, Fenrir was transported out of Asgard to an island somewhere in the nine realms, and a sword was positioned in his jaw to keep his mouth open. Supposedly he is still there to this day and surely quite angry."

"Where was Loki in all of this? If this were his child, wouldn't he try and stop it?"

"That's a good question," said Thyra.

"And the ingredients that went into Gleipnir . . . clearly that's a legend. Those things don't exist."

Thyra shrugged her shoulders.

"Maybe they don't exist because they were all used up making Gleipnir."

Helga stared at Thyra for a moment, then saw Thyra's straight expression shift to a smile. Helga laughed.

"My father Calder told me this story. He said it was passed down to him from my blood parents. I suspect Loki is the one who showed up at Mímisbrunnr that Mimir instructed us to hide from."

"How do you know?" said Helga.

"Odin does not consult with Mimir any longer, and there is a rumor that the Goddess Frigg is confined to Fensalir. If it were Thor, we would have seen lightning or heard thunder . . . which means the last truly fearful Aesir is Loki. Baldr, Hother, and Tyr just do not scare people like the others, and Mimir was shaken. He asked about Fimbulwinter," said Thyra.

"The winter precursor to the end of times. What role does he play in all of this?"

"That is a good question. One that maybe we should look into but as interested as I might be by this, he is not our priority at the moment," said Thyra.

"You're right. We have to stay focused on the task at hand."

"We must stop the three Valkyries from accessing Svartalfheim and Volund from doing whatever evil deeds he has planned."

Thyra put her hands behind her head and lay back on the hard Midgardian soil. She looked up through the dense canopy at the parts of the moon she could see. She thought of Calder, his sister Erika, her husband Ivar, and their child Kari. She thought of her blood parents, Ase and Hagen, whom she never got to know. All of them were gone. She was all that remained of her family.

"Who am I without them?" she whispered.

"What?" said Helga.

"Nothing."

Soon she was asleep. Helga remained vigilant as long as she could but drifted off as well. They slept through the night undisturbed. When they awoke the following day, the fire had died and only embers remained. Little smoke rose from the remnants, and Thyra snuffed it out with dirt.

Helga offered some of the remaining bread from the inn, but Thyra rejected it, so she consumed it herself. The sun was still rising, and morning dew had yet to melt from the ground. The soil crunched underfoot, and their breath was clearly visible.

"Mornings are colder," said Helga.

"Not sure if it's actual winter or this Fimbulwinter," said Thyra.

"Either way, I'm freezing."

She pulled her pelt as close as possible to her body.

"Let us get on with it then. We aren't far from the next hall."

"Wait," said Helga.

"What?"

"Try again."

Thyra looked at her curiously.

"Try projecting your power. Hit that tree over there," she said, pointing behind Thyra. "It's possible we'll meet the Valkyries, and it's definitely likely we'll run into Volund's men. You need to be better prepared."

Thyra turned around and again tried channeling whatever was inside her into the palms of her hands. They warmed and glowed slightly, but she could not release the energy.

"I don't want to state the obvious, but I fear it needs stating. If you cannot master your abilities, you will lose," Helga said.

"I know," said Thyra.

"You have the power. You just have to let it free."

"I know."

"If you don't master your power, then you're going to need to get a lot better with Gambanteinn."

Thyra laughed.

"I'm serious. These Valkyries are out for blood. Dark elf blood specifically."

"I know. At least you're here. I may not need my power with all the strength you seem to pack."

"What do you mean?"

"I mean, you dented elven steel back there. That's no small feat."

"I didn't know I had that in me."

"We are both stronger than we know," said Thyra.

The light elf struggled with his bonds but could not break them despite his strength. The doors of the halls opened, and he looked up to see who was there.

"Volund," he shouted.

"She bested you?" Volund said as he strolled towards the bound elf.

"I'm sorry. There was a child with her. She caught me by surprise."

"A child?" said Volund.

Just then, the light elf knew he said too much. Volund knelt by his side and grabbed the chains in his right hand.

"Beaten by a kid and can't even break iron chains. I must have made a mistake with you."

"Volund, I can make this right."

"You've done enough."

He let go of the chains and took the light elf's head into his hands. With a quick jerk, he snapped his neck and sighed.

Thyra and Helga reached the second hall at midday. Like before, they hitched Sleipnir to a tree and took cover before approaching.

"How do you want to do this?" said Helga.

"I'm thinking."

"I don't see anyone but . . ." said Helga.

"But Volund or his men are probably here."

Helga nodded in agreement.

Thyra scanned the surroundings.

"Stay close," she said, moving from covered position to covered position.

"What are we doing?"

"Footprints or hoofprints. If someone is here, we'll see them."

The two circled the hall and did not find anything that alerted them to another presence.

"Let's check out the hall," said Thyra.

The two quickly scurried to the hall and stopped by one of the windows. Thyra peeked inside.

"Anything?" whispered Helga.

Thyra shook her head.

They moved from the window to the doors. They looked at one another, breathed in deep, and then burst inside. Thyra had her hand on Gambanteinn, but the hall was empty.

"Where are they?" said Helga.

Thyra wiped her finger along the desk to her right. A heavy coating of dust covered it, just like the previous hall.

"The Valkyries aren't here. Let's go before one of Volund's men shows up."

Then as if Thyra and Helga willed it, they heard reigns and the neighing of horses. There were at least two.

"Come out," said one of the riders. "There is nowhere for you to run."

"It was a trap," whispered Thyra.

"One gave us trouble."

Thyra unsheathed her sword. Helga did the same.

"Stay behind me," Thyra said.

Thyra cautiously started for the doors of the hall. Step after step brought her closer to a confrontation, she deep down knew she was not prepared for it but had no choice but to face it. Helga hung close, staying vigilant.

She burst open the doors and standing over her were two light elves on horseback. Their robes flowed over the sides of their horses. Swords hung from their waists.

"Put the weapons down," said the light elf nearest Thyra and Helga.

"Leave us be," said Thyra.

The two light elves laughed and hopped down from their horses. They each had a hand on their swords but had yet to unsheathe them.

"This does not have to be difficult for you," said the light elf nearest Thyra. "Volund enjoys breaking the resistant, so if you come peacefully, maybe it'll work out better for you."

Thyra glanced back at Helga.

"Make up your mind, girl. What's it going to be?"

"Where is Volund?" interjected Helga.

"He's around."

Thyra looked at the two light elves, then once again at Helga.

"We don't have all day, child."

"Helga . . ."

"Yes?"

"Run," shouted Thyra.

Thyra pivoted, and then there was darkness. She did not see the third light elf approaching from the rear. He got the jump on her and Helga.

When she awoke, Thyra found that she was bound back-to-back with Helga, and the three light elves were standing over them conversing. She struggled to get free. The light elves looked her way.

"Try as you might, but you aren't getting free of those chains, and if you use your powers, you'll kill your friend."

"Let us go," shouted Thyra.

The light elves laughed and returned to their conversation.

Thyra nudged Helga.

"Wake up."

Helga stirred and soon regained consciousness.

"Oh no," she said, realizing she was trapped. "Thyra."

"It's ok. It'll be ok."

Helga struggled against the chains, but it was a fruitless endeavor.

Thyra watched the light elves talking amongst themselves.

"They're waiting for Volund," she whispered.

"Trapped like the wolf," said Helga.

"I did not think that story would feel so relevant," whispered Thyra.

"I have an idea," said Helga.

She started to levitate, lifting Thyra with her. The three light elves noticed and did nothing.

"Where do you think you're going?" one said.

Helga and Thyra moved higher but hit an immediate stop. The light elves had tied the chain around part of the hall. The light elves laughed heartily.

"Just give it up. Volund will be here to deal with you two soon enough. Oh . . . I almost forgot."

The light elf walked over and snatched the pouch Thyra had strapped to her person. In it was the piece of the Bifrost key the Valkyries needed.

"Can't forget this?"

"No," shouted Thyra.

"I'll take this to the Valkyries. You two wait for Volund."

The light elves nodded as the one with the key hopped back on his horse.

"Yah," he said, and he was off.

"We have to stop him," said Thyra starting to panic and struggling against her chains.

Her eyes and body started to glow.

"Relax, child. You'll hurt your friend," said one of the light elves.

"I can take it," said Helga. "Break the chains."

The red aura radiated with growing intensity as Thyra clinched her fists and pulled at the chains that bound her wrists. A strong wind whipped up around her and Thyra, making the two light elves' horses retreat to the edge of the trees. The light elves themselves looked at Thyra in horrified amazement.

"What do we do?" the one said.

"I don't know."

The wind intensified as if a powerful storm had just befallen the land. Dirt and small pieces of debris kicked up into the air. Tree branches and loose leaves flew like arrows. The chains stretched at their weak points.

"That is impossible," said one of the light elves.

With a final burst of energy, the chains around her wrists changed color, and Thyra snapped them, freeing her hands. She quickly grabbed the chains at her feet and pried them apart.

"Helga, are you ok?" Thyra shouted over the wind and debris flying about the room.

"I'm fine. Keep it up," shouted Helga.

"That's enough," shouted one of the light elves.

They each had their swords prepared to strike down Helga. Thyra jumped to her feet, grabbed the chain that kept them Midgard bound, and snapped that too.

"Helga, get us out of here," she shouted.

Without hesitation, Helga took to the sky, carrying Thyra with her. One of the light elves leaped after them, but Thyra swatted him away and sent the light elf crashing to the ground.

"Skítur," he said as he got up.

Thyra and Helga disappeared over the cliff nearby and dropped down into the trees below.

"We have to go after them now," said the light elf. "If Volund finds out they got away, we're done."

The two light elves jumped on their horses and made for the path down the cliff.

The red aura dissipated as Helga carried the two of them to the ground.

"Are you ok? Did I hurt you?" said Thyra inspecting Helga as soon as they touched the ground.

"No, I'm fine," said Helga. "Still bound, though."

She held up her chained wrists. Thyra reached out and tried prying them apart, but the power that had freed her a moment ago would not manifest.

"You can do it," said Helga.

Thyra tried, but nothing happened.

"Come on," Helga said. "We're handicapped if I am bound, and the one is on his way back to the Valkyries now. You. Can. Do. This."

"I can do this," said Thyra feeling the warmth of her power grow within her a second time.

It surged from her core into her arms and her hands. It flowed through her legs and into her feet. The wind whipped up around her, and the red aura glowed over her entire body. Helga looked away, for the power was quite intense for such proximity. Like before, the color of the chains around Helga's wrists changed, then strained, stretched, and eventually snapped. Thyra repeated this for the chains around her feet, which also snapped with enough pressure.

"You did it," said Helga. "You controlled your power."

But as soon as she spoke up, the red glow faded, and the wind stopped.

"Not a lot of good it'll do if the light elf reaches the Valkyries with the missing piece of the key. Can you fly us after them?"

"I can levitate at best. Flying is a different story. I won't be able to catch up to a horse, especially one with a significant head start."

"Hmm," said Thyra.

"What do we do?"

She heard the galloping of the two remaining light elves coming down the cliff face path.

"Get ready," said Thyra. "I have an idea."

Moments later

"They're around here somewhere," said one of the light elves. "They could not have gotten far on foot, and I didn't see them take to the sky again. Stay vigilant. We have their weapons, but the dark elf put on quite the display back there."

The light elves remained on horseback but slowed to a trot as they fanned out over the area. Their heads were on a swivel as they looked this way and that for their one-time prisoners.

"Come out, girl. You're only prolonging the inevitable. I told you Volund likes to break the resistant. You're making this harder on yourself than you need to."

The light elves stopped and waited. They looked at one another and then around the forest.

"Where did they go?" one said.

"Come out. This is getting ridiculous."

Just then, the cawing of a massive bird caught the attention of all parties. The two light elves looked up. The bird circled the cliff, then descended to the hall where they were held. From their hiding place, Thyra and Helga could see the fear that befell the light elves.

"Volund," whispered Helga.

Thyra nodded.

"Come out," shouted the light elves with panic in their voices.

"Just as we planned," whispered Thyra to Helga.

Helga nodded and scurried to a group of bushes ahead of the light elves. Thyra remained where she was.

"Hey," shouted Helga as she jumped up from the bushes.

The two light elves immediately directed their attention toward her. As soon as they did, Thyra leaped from her hiding place, holding a massive tree branch. She incapacitated one light elf, but the other got wise to what was happening and attempted to retaliate. But as he did, Helga flew forward and knocked him from the horse with enough force that he slammed into a tree and fell unconscious.

"Get the horses," said Thyra. "I'll grab our swords."

Helga grabbed the reins and hopped on the back of one of the horses. Thyra handed her the sword Helga had taken from the first light elf they encountered, then secured Gambanteinn to her own waist. She got on the second horse and took the reins from Helga.

"We can't let the other get to the Valkyries with the Bifrost," said Thyra. "Yah."

She squeezed the horse with her hips, and it took off. Helga did the same and kept up right behind her.

"Which hall is he going to?" shouted Helga over the sound of the galloping horses.

"There's only one left we haven't visited, and it is in the direction he is headed. That must be where they are," shouted Thyra.

"He's got a significant head start."

"Then we just have to hurry."

Holgor massaged the back of his head as he pulled himself to his feet. He saw Igor still unconscious, but before he went to wake him, the sound of a bird cawing overhead caught his attention.

"Volund," he whispered.

Holgor scrambled for cover as his master descended.

"I'm sorry, Igor," he whispered.

Igor was out cold, but this changed when he felt Volund kick his side. He rolled over onto his back and opened his eyes.

"I must have missed a step when I made your cohort," said Volund. "How are you all being bested?"

"Master," said Igor. "I was . . ."

He was cut off by Volund's boot on his neck.

"Please. No."

Volund put his strength and weight into his boot and crushed Igor's windpipe. He struggled for air but died shortly after.

TWENTY-SEVEN

TAKEN

"Will Sleipnir be ok?" shouted Helga over the sound of their horses galloping through the forest towards the path that would intercept the light elf with the piece of the Bifrost key.

"We'll come back for him," shouted Thyra.

Leaves crunched under the heavy hooves of the two horses, and branches snapped as they raced through the forest. Their pelts danced in the wind.

"The road should be just ahead," shouted Thyra. "But we'll stick to the sides under the canopy."

"Understood."

Seconds later, the road manifested ahead, and just as Thyra instructed, they stuck to the shadows of the canopy. Thyra looked upward to the skies but did not see Volund and his giant bird.

Galloping through the forest had its challenges, and they were not catching up to the light elf with the other piece of the Bifrost.

"This isn't working. We won't catch him this way. I will go ahead on the road. You go get Sleipnir."

"But Thyra, what about Volund? What about Svartalfheim? We need to stick together."

"It's just me he wants. Let me go."

"I'm your flygja. I won't. My sole purpose is your safety."

"That is not your sole purpose, Helga. And besides, I'm safer if I'm not worried about you, which I currently am."

"Thyra, I am here to assist you. To protect you."

"And you will be if you do this for me. If we are captured together, then that is it. The Valkyries will get what they want, and Volund will get what he wants. But if you are still out there, then there is still hope."

"But . . ."

"Listen to your heart. You know I am right."

Helga did not respond immediately but then said, "I will be back."

She stopped her horse and turned around.

"I know you will," Thyra whispered before steering her horse onto the road. She looked back once as Helga moved away from her.

Once on the road, Thyra was much faster. There were no branches to be avoided, bushes that had to be leaped over, and hills to descend or ascend safely. She was nimble and quick. The road was not high-trafficked, so it had its fair share of debris on the path but nothing like an uncharted forest. But being a low-used road was a benefit because the light elf's trail was abundantly clear. She would know which direction he went at forks. Thyra homed in and followed with renewed ferocity.

As she powered down the road, she checked the skies repeatedly. Nothing. Thyra charged ahead. And then she heard it . . . galloping. A few moments later, she saw the light elf come into view. He had not noticed her yet and was galloping along at a slower pace than her. She attempted to close the gap between them, but as she neared, he looked back. His expression was that of concern and curiosity.

"How did you . . . ?" he said. "Yah."

He squeezed his horse and picked up speed. Thyra did the same to keep the gap close. With one hand on the reins and the other on the hilt of Gambanteinn, she unsheathed the sword. The light elf looked back and saw Thyra prepared to fight. He drew his sword as well.

"Give me the key," shouted Thyra.

"You'll have to come and take it."

The light elf squeezed his horse.

"Yah, yah," he shouted.

Thyra was lighter, and her horse was less exhausted. Slowly she closed the gap between the two and came within striking distance. The light elf turned and swung his sword. Thyra parried, creating sparks as the blades clashed. The light elf did not let up. He followed her deflection with a barrage of sword strikes. She defended but fell back, widening the gap between the horses.

"Come on," she shouted.

The light elf steered his horse directly in front of Thyra, so dirt kicked up in her face. She moved left to regain clear sight but had to stop before going over a cliff. The light elf looked back and saw that Thyra had not gone over the edge.

"Damn," he whispered.

Soon enough, she was on the elf's tail again.

"You don't give up so easy," he shouted.

Thyra sheathed the sword and raised her hand towards the light elf. He looked back at her.

"What are you doing?"

"Come on," she whispered.

Thyra felt her palm warming and even saw a slight glow, but ultimately nothing manifested. Thyra grinded her teeth and tried again. Her hand glowed, and then . . . a wave of energy escaped, nearly knocking the light elf from his horse. He looked back, horrified, and stunned. She fired again. He ducked underneath and then turned sharply into the forest that lined the road. Thyra followed.

Within the forest, she retook the reins with both hands as branches and brush came flying at her fast, forcing her to be reactive to random obstacles while pursuing the light elf.

"Volund, where are you?" said the light elf.

The tree line came, and once again, the light elf and Thyra were back on the road. She let go of another blast of energy, and this one connected. The light elf went flying from the horse and tumbled through the dirt, rolling six times before stopping face down.

Thyra slowed her horse to a trot and hopped down when she was just over him to check if he was breathing. He was.

"Where is it?" she whispered, flipping him over.

He was moaning and groaning. His white and black robe was covered in dirt.

"Where is the key?" said Thyra.

"Quite the display you put on."

A shiver found its way down Thyra's spine. She stood up straight and slowly turned around. Without seeing him, she knew who stood behind her.

"Volund," she whispered.

"The nine realms can be predictable, but every so often, something comes along that disturbs that predictability."

Thyra raised her palm to Volund and fired, but he lifted a spear that absorbed the energy.

"That is what I'm talking about. Your lineage is special. And yet the most your father could ever do was just that. Do you know what he lacked?"

Thyra did not answer.

"Imagination," he said.

A beam of rainbow light shone down on Thyra and Volund.

"No," she shouted.

But it was too late. She was gone from Midgard, and so was he.

Helga saw the rainbow touch ground far off in the distance as she neared Sleipnir. Immediately she was overcome by a strange feeling of disconnectedness.

"Something bad has happened," she whispered.

Holgor removed the map of Midgard from his pouch.

"I can be free."

Holgor looked up at the hall atop the hill and started the arduous climb.

TWENTY-EIGHT

TOO LITTLE, TOO LATE

Helga watched the rainbow disappear and exactly knew what had happened. Thyra was en route to Alfheim, which meant that the light elf would get the Bifrost key to the Valkyries.

Sleipnir was where they had left him hours ago—tied to a tree, patiently gnawing on grass. As she approached, he looked up at her. Helga hopped off the horse she had commandeered and walked the rest of the way. Sleipnir neighed when she reached him and rubbed his neck.

"I'm sorry we left you," she said as she untied him from the tree.

"Don't take that horse," said a man behind Helga.

She turned around quickly, taking hold of her sword.

"I'm not going to hurt you," said Holgor. "But I came for the horse."

"You're one of the light elves that attacked us," shouted Helga.

She stepped between him and Sleipnir.

"I am not here to fight," he said. "I just need a horse. Which there are two of."

"Why should I trust you?" said Helga, still holding her sword at attention.

"Igor is dead, and Ove might be beyond my reach, but I just want to be free."

"Ove?" said Helga letting down her guard just a bit.

"The one who left with the piece of the key."

"Why the change of heart?"

170

"No change of heart, just a change of circumstance. I want to be free, and now I can."

"Change of circumstance?"

"I saw the Bifrost bridge. I know he has your friend."

"That's because of you," said Helga.

"It was inevitable."

"Because of your actions."

"I . . . we had no choice."

"How can I trust you?"

Holgor removed his sword from his waist and tossed it at Helga's feet.

"Volund has what he wants, and I just want to disappear into Midgard."

"And Ove . . . does he feel the same way as you?"

"I'm sure."

"Then help me stop him from giving the Bifrost key to the Valkyries. Volund already has Thyra. We can't let Hildr, Svipul, and Gunnr take the dark elves too."

"He's surely already reached the Valkyries. Besides, I want to disappear. I said nothing about intervening," said Holgor. "That would be the exact opposite of what I want."

"Think of it as an opportunity to repent for the Great War. And you will get to save one more of your friends. I doubt the Valkyries care as much about him as you do."

Holgor sighed.

"You're assuming that I want to repent for the Great War. First, I wasn't there. I am of a different cohort. And second, I owe the dark elves nothing. I just want to get away from Volund."

"Why do you want to get away from him so bad? He's made you strong."

"He tortured us. Experimented on us. Threatened our families. We are not this way by choice."

"And you'd let that happen to Thyra?"

Holgor didn't respond immediately.

But then he said, "Yes. This isn't my fight."

"But it is. It's all our fight. Like Volund, the Valkyries are just more tyrants."

"I'm sorry for your friend, but I am out. You can have that horse; just give me the other."

"No."

"Child, I can just take the horse from you."

"I know you can. And I can try and stop the other light elf by myself, but with your help, it's more likely we can change things for the better. Would your life be different if someone had helped you?"

Holgor thought back to when Volund took him from his family's home as a child—how Volund threatened his family when he tried to escape the first time and how he killed his brother when Holgor tried to escape a second time.

"I'll help you stop Ove. But if he's already reached the Valkyries, then you and the dark elf are on your own."

"Deal. Now let's go. We don't have much time."

Helga levitated onto the back of Sleipnir, and Holgor mounted the horse Helga was originally riding. They made for the road and hoped they could catch Ove before he made it to the Valkyries.

"What does Volund want with Thyra?" asked Helga as the two rode after Ove.

"He is obsessed with achieving godhood. It intrigued him during the Great War, and it is why he experimented on the Vanir at his hall."

"Is that where he took her? His hall from the war?"

"Yes."

"Is there a way to save her?"

"He'll keep her alive, but only because he failed to unlock her father's power when he killed him."

"I have to find a way there."

"You'll have to do that yourself."

"I know. You're only helping to stop Ove, and then you're gone."

"It's probably wise you forget about her and just focus on stopping the Valkyries."

Thyra thrashed about as much as she could against her bonds, but it was a fruitless effort. She could not move her arms or legs, which were tied in a thin chain stronger than anything she had ever experienced. Her mouth was gagged with a cloth and tied with the same chain.

"You will only tire yourself out, girl. Don't you know what you're bound in?"

Thyra muffled, "Gueepnir."

Volund laughed.

"Yes. Gleipnir. If it is strong enough for Fenrir. It should be strong enough for you."

As soon as Thyra arrived in Alfheim, Volund was waiting to bind her. She did not know how he got the jump on her since they teleported simultaneously, but somehow, he did it and here she was. Volund wheeled Thyra on a small, human-size cart through a massive hall. She looked left and saw a large squirrel lying belly down on a wooden table with his four paws pinned to the table and a muzzle over his mouth.

"Ratatoskr," said Volund as they passed.

She locked eyes with the squirrel as they went by.

"He can generate a Bifrost bridge without a key, but not while certain pressure points are blocked. Like you, his secrets will be unlocked in time," said Volund as he and Thyra entered through two doors into a small room with a table in the center.

He pushed Thyra to the edge of the table and lifted her from the cart onto the table. She struggled against his grip, but it was to no avail. She could not break the bonds of Gleipnir.

"The chain was a gift from Thor during the Great War. I was able to replicate it through a process I learned while traveling. It's the same process through which I hope to discover your secrets."

Thyra felt Volund secure the chains that bound her to the table. She could see from the corner of her eyes that Volund turned to a cabinet along the wall. He returned to her with a small jug and a knife.

"We'll start with the basics. Your blood."

Thyra's body started to glow, but it quickly dissipated. Though she'd gained some mastery over her powers, they were failing her again.

"You don't know what makes Gleipnir unique, do you? It's not so strong it is unbreakable. No, it simply makes the bound weak."

One hour later

Thyra felt woozy. She had given up a lot of blood, and her body felt drained, figuratively and literally. She looked to her left at the line of blood flowing from her arm. Volund walked over and patched up her arm.

"Don't worry. You're not going to die. That was the mistake I made with your father."

He removed the gag from her mouth, lifted her head, and helped her drink some water.

"Why . . . are you . . . doing this?"

"Because you've been gifted something that I worked years to learn, and you scoff at it."

"I don't . . . even . . . know what . . . this is."

"You're only helping make my point."

Volund carried away the blood he collected, leaving Thyra alone in the well-lit room. She looked around as best she could. The devices hung from the wall were unlike anything she had ever seen. There were serrated short swords, cuffs, a tiny knife that Volund used to make the incision in her arm, tubes, and many other devices she struggled to describe.

"What is this place?" she whispered, slowly regaining some sense of self since her arm had been patched.

"I call it the Alexandria Room," said Volund, returning from storing her blood. "It is one of many in my great hall."

"What?"

"Never mind. You wouldn't understand."

"Who else is here? What else is here?"

Volund smiled and laughed.

"I am proud of my collection," he said.

Volund grabbed the serrated short sword off the wall. Thyra's eyes got wide.

"What are you going to do with that?"

"Your blood is not enough. I need tissue samples as well."

"Wait, wait, wait," said Thyra. "Stop."

Volund dropped the serrated sword to his side.

"What?"

"You don't have to do this," she said.

Volund laughed again.

"Don't worry; I won't maim you . . . for now, just a finger will do."

Volund took Thyra's hand, but she clenched it into a fist. With the hilt of the sword, he smashed the back of her fist, forcing her hand open. He quickly grabbed her little finger and removed it with a few quick strokes. Thyra grinded her teeth together at the pain, but she did not let a tear escape her eyes.

Volund held the finger in front of Thyra's face and laughed.

"If only your father had just submitted to me, you wouldn't be going through this, so really this is his fault."

"You're a monster."

"Those of us who are so forward thinking are often regarded as such."

"What does that mean?"

"It means I see the potential in you, but there is work that must be done to bring it out, and unfortunately for you, I doubt it'll be pleasant."

"Do you . . . know what this power is?"

"Of course, I know. It's transmutation."

"What?"

"It is the act of changing from one state of being to another. It is the core of alchemy."

Thyra arched her head up to look at Volund. Her curiosity was piqued despite the pain stemming from her hand.

"In Odin's hall, they speared her. But she lived, so they burned her, yet she was reborn. They burned her again, but twice she was reborn. So, in their infinite wisdom, the Aesir burned her a third time, and thrice she was reborn. But upon her third rebirth, she wielded a powerful form of seidr magic, unlike anything the Aesir had seen before. For years I thought she was a Vanir god, because the Aesir's treatment of this woman eventually started the Great War. But in time, I learned she was not of Vanaheim, but rather . . . Svartalfheim."

"She was a dark elf?" whispered Thyra.

"Her name was Gullveig. She was your grandmother."

Helga and Holgor were speeding down the road, their horses galloping as fast as they could muster. Wind raced over them both.

"We should have caught up to him by now," said Helga.

"Look," said Holgor pointing ahead of them.

Helga saw the disheveled dirt and the scattered hoof prints.

"He went down here."

"Ove," shouted Holgor.

"Ove, are you near?" shouted Helga.

"He fears Volund more than the rest of us. He would finish his task."

"Let's go then."

They did not waste more time inspecting the crash site and were back on the road at top speed.

"One more should do it," said Volund as he removed Thyra's ring finger.

"Go to Hel," she shouted as blood spewed from her hand.

Volund quickly bandaged her wounds.

"You've lost enough blood," he laughed.

Thyra looked at her damaged hand.

"You're sick."

"Your grandmother was the greatest sorcerer the nine realms have ever known because she knew what she was. Even your father was a skilled warrior, but what are you? You're neither. I will give you a purpose, though. You will help me figure out how I can make your power, my power."

"You'll . . . pay . . . for this," whispered Thyra.

"Here," he said, putting a piece of cod to her lips. "I think it's time you ate. I'll need you strong enough for round two."

Thyra took a bite and spit it at Volund. It splattered across his face. He wiped the bits of fish off him and took a deep breath.

"One of my other experiments was defiant too. I carved up members of his family in front of him. He was more agreeable afterward. I saw from the sky the girl you were traveling with. It would be no problem at all to bring her here."

Reluctantly Thyra took a bite of the cod.

"That's more like it."

"I see him," shouted Helga as she and Holgor rounded a corner.

Ove was charging ahead. But just beyond him, far in the distance, was the Valkyries' hall.

"Ove, stop," shouted Helga.

He looked back at her and Holgor. Bewilderment spread across his face. Then he pulled on the reins of his horse and waited for Helga and Holgor to catch up.

"What is going on here?" he said to Holgor.

"We don't need to do this," said Holgor. "Volund has the girl. We don't have to give the Valkyries the Bifrost key."

"But . . ."

"Do the right thing," said Helga. "If Thyra is lost, you can at least save her people."

Ove looked at Holgor. Holgor nodded.

"Save her people? I don't care about them."

"We can choose a different path. We can stay here in Midgard."

Ove looked at Helga, then took out the piece of the Bifrost key from his satchel. He played with it in his hand.

Helga watched him, but something caught her eyes. She shifted her focus skyward, and incoming was Hildr and Svipul.

"No," she whispered.

"Where is Igor?" said Ove.

"Volund," said Holgor.

"And Canute?"

"Is that who attacked us first? We tied him up. He is ok," said Helga.

"If you beat him, then he is probably dead too," said Ove. "Holgor, you know what Volund is capable of. You know what he did to my family."

"I know."

"Ove, we are out of time," said Helga watching Hildr and Svipul approach.

Ove and Holgor took notice that her attention was elsewhere and looked up.

"I have to finish this," said Ove.

"If you give them the piece of the key, then innocents are going to die," said Helga.

"Innocents have already died. I have one child left. I can't risk him."

He turned his horse around and jerked the reins.

"Yah," he shouted.

"Ove, no," shouted Helga.

Helga watched Hildr and Svipul descend from the sky, land in front of Ove, and stop his horse abruptly. Helga made eye contact with Hildr, who was smiling.

"You have something for me?" she said to Ove.

He handed her the piece of the key. She took it into her hand and looked back at her sister.

"We're going to be ok."

"Where is Volund?" said Svipul.

"According to them," said Ove gesturing towards Helga and Holgor. "Alfheim with the dark elf."

"You've done well," said Hildr.

With that, she flapped her mighty wings and took to the sky.

"What will become of her?" said Svipul.

"Nothing pleasant," said Ove.

"Hmph."

Helga watched the exchange and saw Svipul look past Ove at her.

"Tell her I'm sorry," said Svipul.

TWENTY-NINE

GET FREE

Thyra rested on the table, having consumed enough food and water to regain some of her strength. She looked around the room, unsure of what she hoped to find. Nothing had changed. She tried to manifest her powers again, and just like the room, it was still the same. She was stuck, in pain, missing two fingers on her left hand, and still too much blood from her body.

"I can't die here," she whispered.

"You're not going to die here," said Volund, appearing at the end of the table. "I'll keep you alive. Don't fret."

"Why are you doing this?"

"The Aesir promised me and my fellow light elves godhood, and they reneged on that promise. But I am going to find my own way to achieve it."

"Through torture?"

"Through alchemy. If one thing can be learned from humans, it is that using your mind can help you overcome many challenges. The first alchemist is rumored to have been a human. But even if humans founded it, I mastered it by looking beyond our realms, and I will ascend through my mastery of this art. I just need the proper ingredients . . . you."

"The gods will never accept you. You will always be an outsider to them."

Volund laughed. "I don't care about being accepted. What sort of fool cares about acceptance? No, they won't accept me. But they will respect me."

Volund leaned over Thyra. He pulled her eyelids back and looked into her eyes. He put his fingers to her neck and checked her pulse.

"You seem rested enough. Now the real fun begins. You probably wondered why I took your fingers."

"Not exactly," said Thyra.

"I had to make sure I had the proper tools on site to sustain parts of your body without them being attached to you. Everyone has a different physiological makeup. You especially. I did not want to risk anything larger than a finger. But it seems I have what I need, so now we can get to work. Your power flows throughout your entire body. You are unique because, unlike most creatures with power, yours does not stem from the World Tree as it does for magic wielders or Valkyries; it comes from inside of you like the gods. The best way for me to tap into that is a piece at a time. I'll start with a leg."

Volund grabbed the serrated sword from the tabletop behind him.

"No, no, no, no stop," shouted Thyra as she squirmed within Gleipnir.

"I must confess, this is going to hurt."

He placed the blade on the top of Thyra's right thigh and started to saw.

Thyra roared, "No."

And the room started to shake. Volund pulled back in disbelief.

"This is impossible."

Her body glowed a bright crimson red, and Gleipnir glowed gold. The room fell to shambles as Volund backed away from the table.

"How are you doing this?"

Thyra sat up and expanded her arms. The chain that bound her expanded and broke.

"That's impossible," he whispered.

Thyra turned towards him and leaped from the table. Volund stepped backward until he hit the wall and could not go any further.

"You really are something special," he whispered.

"I should kill you," said Thyra.

"But you won't," he said. "Mercy. A weakness that will be exploited."

She pressed up against his chest. Thyra grabbed his neck.

"Do it," he said.

She tightened her grip.

"You killed my parents. You slaughtered my people."

"And I tortured you. Don't forget that."

Thyra exhaled through her nostrils. A wave of energy exploded from her, destroying the room, sparing only Volund.

"I can see the conflict in you. Kill me or let me live. Power over others is intoxicating, especially over those who have done you wrong, but you're scared of who you would become if you exerted that power."

"I'm not scared of who I would become. But I am scared of who I am."

Thyra grinded her teeth.

"I won't kill you."

"I knew it. You're . . ."

A sudden pain shot through Volund's body.

"I'll just disable you," she said.

Volund looked down and saw that Thyra had kicked and broken his left ankle. She repeated this on his right ankle, then let go of him, and he fell to the ground.

"Mercy is not a weakness," she said and ran out of the room.

Volund lay on the ground with his broken ankles and crawled over to the tattered Gleipnir chain. He took it into his hands, inspected it, and laughed.

"She is phenomenal."

Thyra ran through the passages of Volund's hall towards Ratatoskr. Light elves disturbed by the explosion in Volund's laboratory emerged from various rooms.

"What is going on?" some were saying.

"A dark elf."

"How did she get here?"

Thyra ignored them and kept running towards where she remembered Ratatoskr to be.

"Someone stop her."

A light elf leaped in front of Thyra with a sword, but with a wave of her hand, her red aura sent the light elf through a wall. A few other light elves saw this and stepped out of her way.

"Ratatoskr," shouted Thyra.

Ratatoskr, resigned to his fate, ignored the commotion, but upon hearing his name, he looked up.

"Has someone come to save me?" he said. "I'm here. Hear my voice."

Thyra heard the squirrel and adjusted her path accordingly.

"I'm coming," she shouted.

Thyra turned the corner, and there was Ratatoskr still pinned to the table.

"We're getting out of here," she said.

She reached for one of the pins, and before she removed it, Volund, who had somehow caught up to her, said, "I wouldn't."

Thyra turned around to face him. He was standing just fine, despite having his ankles broken moments ago.

"I thought . . ."

"I haven't been experimenting for all these years just to empower others."

"How do I free Ratatoskr?"

"Those pins are connected to his nervous system, which controls his ability to generate a Bifrost bridge. Remove those the wrong way, and you could damage him irreparably, stranding you here."

"How. Do. I. Free. Him?"

"You don't," said Volund.

Thyra looked back at the squirrel.

"You have made your scene; now, let's get back to work," said Volund.

Thyra stepped back.

"Ratatoskr, if I make a mistake and you lose your ability, I will defend you to the death."

"I'll hold you to that."

Thyra reached for the first pin.

"No," shouted Volund.

Thyra unleashed a wave of energy at Volund, sending him flying. She quickly turned around and delicately pulled the first pin from Ratatoskr's paw.

"How do you feel?"

"Fine, but you better hurry. He is getting up."

Thyra wiped a bead of sweat from her brow and grabbed the second pin. Slowly she removed it. Ratatoskr's front two paws were free.

"Thank you. Thank you," he said, rubbing his paws together for the first time in hours. "I thought I would be here forever."

Volund watched as Thyra removed the third pin.

"This isn't over," he whispered.

Volund disappeared.

"He's gone," said Ratatoskr as Thyra extracted the final pin. "What is with that guy?"

"How do you feel?" said Thyra.

"Better now. Where do you need to go?"

"Midgard. The hall of Hildr."

"I was hoping not to see those Valkyries again, but seeing how you just saved me, I guess it is the least I can do. Take my paw."

Thyra grabbed hold.

"And we're off," said Ratatoskr as a rainbow formed around them.

THIRTY

NO TIME FOR SENTIMENTALITY

Saga took a powerful, wide stance, ax drawn. Calmness consumed her as she let her troubles wash away. She let out a deep sigh and swung her ax. With a single strike, Saga felled a medium-size tree. Its branches snapped on its way to the forest floor and landed with a thud.

"You're getting good at that. It takes me at least two swings," said Jarl, who appeared behind her.

She turned around and smiled.

"That is because you are lazy," she said.

Jarl laughed.

"I might have slacked, but why bother training so hard when I have you."

They kissed.

"My brother would not approve of your laziness."

"Your brother is paranoid. No offense."

"He remembers the Great War."

"So do I."

"He was older than you."

"So, I will train more . . . we can be the most skilled warriors who never fight a battle."

"Give me your hands."

Jarl held out his hands. Saga took them into hers and touched his palms.

"Soft," she said. "You really haven't been practicing."

"Saga, nothing is going to happen here. It's been 200 years since the Great War, and it's been peaceful this entire time. I don't know why Hakon insists we train like we do. Plus, we have that shield around Svartalfheim, so the only visitors will only ever be other dark elves."

"Not smart," she said.

"Moving on," said Jarl. "I came to tell you that my mother wishes to have us over for dinner.

Saga held out the ax.

"What do you want me to do with that?"

"Help me cut up this tree, and I will join you and Iona."

She waved it in front of him.

"Come on, let's form some callouses on those smooth hands."

"We aren't going to be out here all night doing this," he said.

"We'll stop when you form five blisters, and then we'll meet up with your mom."

Jarl looked at Saga with a straight face, then snatched the ax.

"Now put that anger to good use."

"It seems your sister and my brother have grown quite fond of each other over the years," said Hillevi. "Does that make our relationship weird?"

Hakon turned from the window of their small cottage toward his wife.

"There are so few of us left. I don't think any of us have much choice in who we fall in love with."

"So, was I the wife by default?"

"I would have tried to marry you if there were ten billion of us. I got lucky."

"We both did."

A knock at the door shifted their attention from one another. Hakon went to answer it.

"Yes?" he said.

"Sir, I am sorry to bother you, but I saw something impossible," said the woman at the door.

"What is it?"

"Maybe not impossible but certainly improbably."

"Tell me . . . what did you see?" said Hakon.

"I was at the gate, and in the distance, I saw a rainbow."

"A Bifrost," whispered Hakon.

"What is it?" said Hillevi rushing to his side.

"I knew this wouldn't last forever," said Hakon. "No one has traveled to or from Svartalfheim in hundreds of years."

"The only ones who can travel here are other dark elves. Maybe it's ok," said Hillevi.

Hakon looked at Hillevi.

"I don't know. I have a bad feeling about this."

"What is going on?" said the woman at the door.

"Alert all the guards," said Hakon.

"Alert them to what?"

"Just have them be ready," said Hakon. "It could be nothing, but I would rather we be prepared and not have to act than have to act and not be prepared."

The woman nodded and ran off.

"What do you think is going on? You think it's him?" said Hillevi. "The one Hagen warned us of?"

"I hope not. But no one has used a Bifrost around here since Ase and Hagen left, and I doubt they would ever return. Besides, they would have just Bifrost into the town if they did."

Just then, the bells at the gate started ringing. The door to the cottage slammed open a second time. Jarl and Saga were standing in the doorway.

"What's happening?" said Saga.

"We don't know yet," said Hakon.

"But it isn't good?" Saga said.

"We don't know."

"Then why ring the bells?" said Jarl.

"We're just being cautious."

"Valkyries at the gate," shouted a man running down the street. "Valkyries at the gate."

"Valkyries?" said Hakon looking at Hillevi.

"You two stay here," said Hillevi.

"We can help," said Saga.

"There may not be any reason to, and I'd rather you two be here where it's safe," said Hakon.

"We're not children anymore. There is hardly an age difference between us after two hundred years, brother," said Saga.

"But I am responsible for this town, and as its leader, I am instructing you to stay put."

"Let's just listen to him," said Jarl.

"Fine."

Hakon and Hillevi left the cottage and headed straight to the front gate.

"Valkyries only come for the dead," said Hillevi.

"So why are they here?"

Hildr and Svipul walked up to the gate of the lone dark elf town, with Gunnhild bringing up the rear. They each had a hand on their swords but did not intend to draw them. Taking whom they could alive would be preferable, according to Gunnhild.

"We are so close now," whispered Hildr. "I can taste our freedom. It's just behind those walls."

"I will talk to them," said Hakon.

"But what if . . ."

"It's my responsibility."

He kissed Hillevi and approached the gate. Hakon opened a slit in the wall that separated the town from the rest of Svartalfheim.

"Valkyries, what business do you have here? We have no dead to collect."

"It is not the dead we seek," answered Hildr.

"Then what is your purpose here?"

"Let us in," said Hildr.

"I can't do that."

"We can just fly over. Us talking to you is more of a courtesy."

"Our archers are very skilled."

Hildr smiled.

"I am sure they are. Are you the leader of this town?"

"I am. My name is Hakon."

"Hakon, with so few dark elves left in the nine realms, I am going to assume that you would do everything in your power to save your town . . . to save your people?"

"Of course."

"How many live in this town?"

"Why do you ask?"

"How many?" said Hildr.

"That's not important," said Hakon.

"Less than 200, I'm sure—maybe less than 100. Dark elves were truly decimated. Elves don't reproduce like humans, but still, there used to be hundreds of thousands of dark elves, and in the blink of an eye, you were almost all wiped out . . . tragic."

"What is the point of all of this?" said Hakon growing impatient.

"With so few left, you cannot risk a fight where so many might lose their lives, and my sister and I are quite capable warriors. Sure, you may eventually win, but how many of you would be lost? It would be a loss you cannot afford, but I can offer you a way to minimize that loss," said Hildr.

"Did you come here to fight?"

"Not if we don't have to. Do you want to fight?"

Hakon didn't answer. Instead, he said, "What are you suggesting?"

"Give us ten of your people. No fight. No unnecessary loss of life."

"Give you ten of our people?"

Hakon put his hand on his sword and glanced up at the archers. They readied their bows at Hildr, Svipul, and Gunnhild.

"Think for a second," said Hildr. "Ten will save ninety."

"Brother, what is going on?" shouted Saga, running down the hill towards the gate.

"I told you to stay back," he shouted.

"You can save her," said Hildr.

Saga joined Hakon at the gate.

"What do you want, Valkyrie?" said Saga.

"I have this under control, Saga. Go," said Hakon.

She looked at her brother and then at Jarl, who was standing halfway between the gate and Hakon's cottage.

"Are they here for a fight?" she whispered.

Hakon nodded.

"This is what we have been preparing for."

"But there are so few of us," he whispered.

"It's just two Valkyries. How difficult could this be?"

Hildr laughed.

"I can assure you . . . quite difficult."

The Bifrost bridge touched down, and where the rainbow had been stood Thyra holding Ratatoskr. Helga, Holgor, and Ove turned around. A smile spread across Helga's face.

"I thought I'd lost you," she said.

"What's going on here?" said Thyra looking past Helga at the two light elves.

"They're ok," said Helga. "Volund made slaves of them. But Ove . . ."

"But Ove what?"

"He did give the Valkyries the piece of the Bifrost. Apparently, Volund . . ."

"I know," said Thyra holding up her hand and missing fingers.

"He is a sadist," shouted Ove.

"How did you get here?" said Helga.

"That would be because of me," said Ratatoskr.

"He can generate Bifrost bridges without a key," said Thyra. "He can take us to Svartalfheim to warn them of the Valkyries."

"I did not agree to that," said Ratatoskr.

"What about the magic that protects Svartalfheim?" said Holgor.

"What do you mean?" said Thyra.

"The Valkyries wanted your key because a powerful spell protects Svartalfheim from outsiders, aka those who are not dark elves," said Holgor.

"That is true," added Ratatoskr.

"But I am with you," Thyra said.

"It doesn't work like that," Ratatoskr said. "Your people were gifted unique keys, and I am not one of them. Besides, I never said I was doing this. I don't want to get any more involved than I already am."

"Ratatoskr, it is not fair for me to ask you, but we need your help."

"I must be a fool," Ratatoskr said.

"Give me your paw."

Ratatoskr did as she said.

"I spent quite some time with the gem that powered my Bifrost. Perhaps I can share its unique properties with you."

"If you can do that, then you are something special indeed."

Thyra's hand closed around Ratatoskr's paw and glowed red. Ratatoskr glowed gold.

"Is it working?" Holgor said.

"Only one way to find out," said Thyra.

"Will you take us to Svartalfheim?" said Helga. "Time is not on our side. The Valkyries left ten minutes ago."

Ratatoskr looked around at the eclectic group and sighed again.

"Each of you, grab on to one another, and dark elf, you hold onto me," he said. "Let's find out how powerful you are."

"Hey, you two," said Helga. "This is a great opportunity to do some good."

"I told you. I'm not helping you with the dark elves."

"Then why haven't you gone already?" said Helga.

Holgor and Ove locked eyes, and Holgor slapped Ove's knee.

"Come on," he said.

"But . . ."

"We have to try and make things right."

Ove looked at the ground for a moment, then shook his head.

"I know what Volund did Ove, but . . ."

"No, you don't."

"You can stay here," said Thyra.

Ove looked up at her.

"Volund is a monster . . . I'm . . . scared . . . not for my own safety but for . . ."

"Your son will always be in danger as long as Volund is alive," said Holgor.

Ove looked Holgor's way.

"Let's be better than our parents," said Holgor.

Ove sighed, "Fine," he said.

Holgor helped him to his feet.

"It'll be all right."

"It better."

Thyra watched the two light elves run over their way.

"After what happened during the Great War, I never thought I would see the day," said Ratatoskr. "Light elves and a dark elf holding hands."

"No time for sentimentality," said Helga.

"You're no fun. Let's be off," said Ratatoskr.

THIRTY-ONE

THE SECOND ASSAULT ON SVARTALFHEIM

Smoke plumes rose high into the Svartalfheim sky as the last dark elf town burned.

"How could we be this ill-prepared for battle after all these years?" said Hillevi as she scoured the skies for the attacking Valkyries.

"We were prepared," said Hakon. "That's Hildr and Svipul. Their skills are legendary."

"Well prepared or not, we are losing."

"I know. You need to get everyone out of here."

"We . . . need to get everyone out of here," said Hillevi.

"No. I will distract them as best I can. You take everyone you can to the tunnels."

"Brother, what did you say?" said Saga running to Hakon's side.

"Talk some sense into him," said Hillevi. "He plans to sacrifice himself."

"This is a battle we won't win," said Hakon.

Hildr and Svipul passed overhead. Hakon, Hillevi, and Saga turned their bows skyward and unleashed a barrage of arrows. None connected.

"They will whittle us down then pick off the ten they want," said Saga.

"Meanwhile, our town burns and dark elf lives hang in the balance," said Jarl. "Just give them the ten."

"Are you offering yourself?" said Hakon.

"Jarl?" shouted Saga.

"The longer this goes on, the more precarious our situation becomes. We can avoid having to flee and the destruction of our town if we just let them have what they want."

"And again, I ask . . . will you be offering yourself?"

"Look at them," said Hildr. "They fight amongst themselves."

"Their defenses are broken, and their people scattered. We can start picking them off," said Svipul.

"Jarl, we can't just surrender our people," said Saga. "What's come over you?"

"I don't want what we built to be crushed before it has a chance to survive."

"And yet you did not train to fight," shouted Saga.

"That would not make the difference here."

"It could . . ."

Saga could not finish her statement. Hildr swooped in, grabbed her by the collar of her pelt, and lifted her into the sky. The sudden jerk caused Saga to drop her sword. Hildr carried her to Gunnhild unarmed.

"One down, nine to go. Bind her," said Hildr, hitting Saga on the back of the head, so she fell unconscious.

Hildr took off again, back towards the town. Gunnhild proceeded to bind Saga's hands and feet. Saga stirred and opened her eyes.

"You . . . don't have to do this," she said.

"It is too late. I'm sorry," she said and shrugged.

From a distance, Hakon, Hillevi, and Jarl saw more dark elves swept up by the Valkyries.

"We have to get Saga," shouted Jarl.

"They're flying beyond the gates," said Hillevi. "They brought a human with them."

"A human?" said Jarl. "Then let's go get her now."

"Think, brother. If they're leaving them with a human, there is a reason. She surely is not just . . ."

An explosion cut her off. The three dark elves looked towards the gate and ran to one of the archers' perches. Looking down below, they could see the cindering remains of one of their fellow townspeople. It looked as though he had been running to attack Gunnhild.

"That human is a rune writer. A skilled practitioner of seidr magic. Attacking her won't be easy."

"We can't do nothing," said Jarl.

"Valkyries overhead. A rune writer guarding our captured," said Hakon.

He looked out over the town he helped shepherd for almost two centuries. It was on fire. A tear came to his eye.

"Hillevi, take Jarl and as many of us as possible and evacuate. There are tunnels underground," said Hakon. "I will do what I can to hold them off."

"No," said Hillevi.

"There is no other choice."

She hesitated for a moment, then subtly nodded.

"I love you," she said.

"I love you, too."

"Come on, Jarl, you coward bastard. We have work to do."

Hakon picked up the bow of one of the downed archers and loaded an arrow.

"Be safe," he said to Hillevi and Jarl.

Hildr and Svipul landed by Gunnhild after she exploded the approaching dark elf.

"Try not to kill them," said Hildr. "We need them alive. You said that."

"Hurry and finish things. All your efforts will be for naught if one of these dark elves harms or kills me."

"We'll wrap this up shortly," said Svipul. "Come, sister, we promised to spare as many as possible."

Hildr nodded and took off after Svipul.

"Go now," shouted Hakon to Hillevi and Jarl as he spied Hildr and Svipul take flight.

He turned his bow towards them and rapidly unloaded arrow after arrow. Hillevi and Jarl climbed back to the ground and started gathering folks from within their homes, directing them towards the tunnel passageways connected to each home.

Hillevi spied the two Valkyries reach Hakon despite his display of archery prowess. They knocked him from his perch, and he hit the ground below with a thud and did not get up.

"Keep helping the people," she said to Jarl.

He nodded and ran off.

Hillevi unsheathed her sword and started running towards her husband, and the two Valkyries hovered over him.

"Leave him alone," she shouted.

Svipul picked up Hakon and threw him over her shoulder. She flapped her massive wings and took to the sky.

"Look around you," said Hildr. "Your town is burning, and we are picking off your people with ease. It's over. Give it up."

"Never," said Hillevi.

"Fools."

Then just as the two were about to clash, the boom of a Bifrost bridge caught both their attention.

Helga, Ove, Holgor, Ratatoskr, and Thyra touched down in Svartalfheim outside the gate of the last dark elf town, and the first thing they all noticed was the plumes of smoke rising into the sky.

"Are we too late?" whispered Helga.

Thyra scanned the landscape.

"This is Svartalfheim," she whispered to herself.

Helga touched Thyra's shoulder. Thyra looked at her.

"Ready?" said Helga.

Thyra nodded and turned towards the wall that surrounded the town.

"Holgor and Ove, you help the people here evacuate the town. Bring them here to Ratatoskr. Helga, I want you to find those who have been taken. We can all hear the chaos inside the town, so the Valkyries are still here, and chances are, so are their captives. Once you find them, join Holgor and Ove. I am going to confront the Valkyries."

"Got it," said Holgor and Ove in unison.

"How do you propose to confront the Valkyries?" said Helga.

"I'll figure it out."

"Figure it out quickly, and . . . good luck," said Helga. "Come on, you two, let's get out of here."

The three took off to complete their respective missions.

When they were gone, Ratatoskr said, to Thyra, "If you all aren't back here in fifteen minutes, I'm leaving."

"I understand."

Thyra took off towards the gate.

Hildr and Hillevi turned their attention towards the gate as Thyra slipped inside.

"Get out of here," shouted Hillevi.

"You're too late," said Hildr. "Go home if you don't want to die."

"You can still stop this," said Thyra.

Hillevi looked at Thyra curiously.

Svipul landed behind Thyra as she approached Hildr and Hillevi. She glanced back at the second Valkyrie. Smoke and fires raged all around them.

"Stop what you are doing and leave," said Thyra.

"Too little too late. You've lost," said Hildr.

A red aura worked its way up Thyra's body. Hillevi took a step back, realizing that perhaps all participants in the impending fight were out of her league.

"Help the others," said Thyra to Hillevi.

Hillevi nodded and pivoted.

"You mastered your powers. Good for you. You're still too late," said Hildr.

Hildr gestured at Svipul. She took flight and charged for Thyra. Thyra turned and unleashed a wave of energy that sent Svipul tumbling to the ground. But it was a distraction. Hildr was on top of Thyra and swinging for her with her sword. The blade made contact against her right arm and immediately turned to steam, to everyone's surprise, but Thyra's.

Hildr dropped the hilt, all that remained of the blade, and leaped backward.

"What was that?" she said.

Svipul pulled herself to her feet.

"Impossible," she whispered.

"Leave these people alone," said Thyra.

"What are you?" shouted Hildr.

Thyra took a step towards Hildr, and she took a step back.

Svipul felt the sword in her hand. She considered briefly trying to attack again but decided against it. What could she do that her sister could not?

"Hildr, let's go," shouted Svipul.

"No. We have come too far."

"Listen to your sister," said Thyra. "I'm giving you a way out; despite all you have done."

Hildr grinded her teeth and clenched her fists.

"Fine," she said defiantly. "We'll go."

"I will follow you back to Midgard, and you will give me the Bifrost key," said Thyra.

Hildr nodded.

"Sure," she said.

Helga spied Gunnhild under a tree with her captive dark elves hog-tied at her feet. She looked around and did not see the Valkyries.

"Just a human?" said Helga rhetorically.

She unsheathed her sword and began her approach. Gunnhild saw her immediately.

"A child?" she whispered.

Helga did not speak. She quickly turned her sword to strike and started running towards Gunnhild. Helga's approach caught Gunnhild by surprise, but she promptly responded by holding up a small rock with a carving on it. A bolt of lightning struck down from the sky, electrifying Helga.

For a moment, everything was at a standstill, and all she saw was a blinding white light. Her entire body ached. She had to jab her sword into the ground to give herself support to stand up.

"Impossible," said Gunnhild.

Helga looked up at Gunnhild.

"What are you?" Gunnhild said.

"A flygja."

"Thyra's, I assume."

Helga nodded.

Gunnhild examined Helga, then said, "Take the dark elves. We will leave you."

Svipul and Hildr heard the explosion caused by the lightning bolt.

"Who was with you?" said Hildr.

Thyra did not respond.

"Thyra, you are powerful, but what do you hope to achieve? If it's not us, it'll just be someone else."

"That does not mean I should let you do my people wrong."

"Your people? You were born in Midgard. You have some sort of special power that I have never seen any other dark elf display. These are as much your people as the Aesir are mine," said Hildr.

"Think what you will, Valkyrie, but stopping you is the right thing to do."

"You're self-righteous, and that'll get you killed in the nine realms."

Just then, Gunnhild appeared in front of them.

"I know what she is."

"What am I?"

The boom of a Bifrost reverberated through the town. Thyra noticed Hildr, Gunnhild, and Svipul direct their attention behind her, so she turned around.

Standing in the center of town was Volund. He was wearing an artfully crafted, armored pelt, and attached to his waist was a massive broadsword. An equally artful helmet covered his face, but his eyes were visible and trained on Thyra.

"Thyra Olufgullveig, I have come for you," he announced.

"Impossible," said Thyra. "He should not be able to access this realm."

Gunnhild took advantage of Thyra's distraction and gestured for the two Valkyries to come near. They did so.

"You heal fast," said Thyra.

"I have Valkyries to thank for that."

"That's why his men knew the location of our halls," said Hildr.

"Gunnr knew better than to work with him."

"He will distract her, but he won't defeat her. But you can," said Gunnhild to Svipul and Hildr.

"How?" said Hildr.

"We must go to Jotunheim."

Hildr grabbed Svipul and Gunnhild and triggered the Bifrost.

Thyra quickly turned around and shouted "no," but they were already gone.

Volund laughed.

"Did I interrupt things?" he said.

"How are you here?"

"I figured out the spell protecting Svartalfheim a long time ago. I just knew my prize was not here until now."

Then hundreds of Bifrost bridges touched down around the small dark elf town. Light elves poured over the walls.

"Fan out and find the dark elves. If they resist, kill them, but those who don't—bring them to me. I want to show this one here what happens to those who defy me."

The icy winds of Jotunheim were in stark contrast to the warmth of Svartalfheim. It pierced the pelts of the two Valkyries and Gunnhild.

"Why are we here in the land where our sister died?" said Hildr.

"I know what the dark elf is. I know why Volund wants her so bad," said Gunnhild.

"What is she?" said Hildr raising her voice, growing impatient.

Gunnhild paused and said, "Though he may be one of the most skilled, Volund is not the only alchemist. And there is something that they all seek."

"What?"

"You sought me out because I am one of the best rune writers, and I specialize in the tattoos you need. I'm only as good as I am because of my teacher, and she was knowledgeable beyond measure. She knew of Volund and how he learned alchemy in all and beyond the nine realms, and in that land, they call it the Philosopher's Stone."

"The what?" said Svipul."

"Volund said her full name was Thyra Olufgullveig which means she is a descendent of Gullveig, the being thrice reborn after being burned by the Aesir before the Great War. When she was reborn the third time, she could wield seidr magic unlike anything or anyone. Not even the Goddess Frigg, who is responsible for human rune writers, was able to match Gullveig in her ability. Then Gullveig disappeared. It has long been believed by rune writers and alchemists alike that Gullveig's death and rebirth indicate her status as a Philosopher's Stone since it is the key to achieving immortality."

"What does her being a Philosopher's Stone mean?" said Svipul.

"It means that she can make and remake the world as she sees fit. Iron can be made into gold. Steel can become water. Life can never cease."

"If she is all-powerful, what are we to do?" said Hildr.

"Volund will keep her busy and hopefully tire her. And as you know, time moves quicker in Jotunheim. Let me redraw your tattoos, and when they are finished, we return to Svartalfheim, after they have battled, and you finish her. Then no one will be able to stop you from taking the remaining dark elves, Volund's hall will be yours, and we can be done with this mess."

THIRTY-TWO

IT'S IN THYRA'S HANDS NOW

Moments Before Volund Arrived

Holgor and Ove met up with Jarl, who was helping facilitate the evacuation of the dark elf town. The two light elves startled Jarl, who grabbed for his sword upon their approach.

"We came to help," said Holgor.

"Light elves helping dark elves," said Jarl. "That's a laugh. Get out of here. We have enough problems."

"We mean it. What can we do?" said Ove.

"Why are you here?" said Jarl.

"Trying to be better," said Holgor.

Jarl looked them up and down.

"You came here with her?" said Jarl gesturing towards Thyra.

Holgor and Ove each nodded.

At that moment, Hillevi arrived.

"Who are they?" she said, just as startled by the light elves as Jarl had been.

"They came with the glowing dark elf."

Hillevi eyed the light elves and said, "Help guide families into the underground tunnels. Go door to door and make sure everyone is getting out ok and no one is injured."

"We are on it."

Holgor and Ove ran off to do as they were instructed.

"Do you trust them?" said Jarl.

"Do we have a choice right now?"

Right then, a Bifrost touched down in the center of town, and standing where it appeared was Volund.

"Now what?" said Jarl.

Hillevi immediately turned towards Holgor and Ove, who were out of sight.

Then Bifrosts triggered around the town, and light elves started coming over the walls.

"Skítur," whispered Hillevi.

"That is Volund," said Holgor to Ove, who took cover as soon as the Bifrost appeared.

"I knew joining up with the dark elves was a bad idea," said Ove. "I knew it. I should have gone with my gut instinct."

"Pull it together. We aren't his concern."

"No, we're not, but if he knows we're helping the dark elves, we'll incur his wrath."

"That's if he wins here," said Holgor.

"Has he ever lost?" said Ove.

Holgor glanced out at Volund and Thyra.

"This might have been a bad idea."

Thyra stared down at Volund and his fancy armor with the massive spear. A weed tumbling in the wind swept across the space between them.

"I was impressed with your escape," said Volund. "You confirmed what I hoped was true. You turned Gleipnir, one of the most precious and rarest metals in the nine realms, into one of the most brittle of metals, sodium, and broke it. Something not even Fenrir has managed to do."

"Sodium?"

Volund laughed.

"You don't even know what you are doing. You are just acting on instinct. I love it. You are the highest form of an alchemist. You're a Philosopher's Stone."

"And that means what?" said Thyra.

"You can do anything. You are as limited as your imagination. But you have much to learn. Let me help you master your abilities."

"A moment ago, you wanted to cut pieces off of me to experiment," said Thyra holding up her hand. "I think I will decline your offer."

"That was before," said Volund. "Now I know for sure. With your natural ability and my years of expertise, we can do great things."

"You're asking me to join you. That's laughable," said Thyra.

Volund chuckled.

"It was worth a shot."

He raised his hand and twirled his finger. The light elves he brought with him started raiding the homes of the dark elves, dragging those who had not made it underground out into the streets. Thyra darted forward towards Volund, but he raised his hand, and she stopped.

"I wouldn't do that," he said.

The light elves put swords to the necks of those they captured.

"There are two ways we can proceed," he said. "The first is you attack me. We engage in a back and forth, and you ultimately win. I know when someone is stronger than me. But while we fight, my men slaughter what remains of your people. You get to live, but everything you fought for up to this point dies. The second way we can proceed is you drop your guard and come with me so that I can continue my experiments. I know you'll never work by my side, but I can try to harness that power inside you. I'll leave some of my men here for insurance, but your people will get to live, and as an added bonus, I'll take care of those two Valkyries for you, so you can rest assured that your people are ok. How does that sound?"

"So, it's my people or me," said Thyra.

"Thyra, you want to play hero, but that is a role fit just for fools. Your parents thought they were heroes, and look where it got them. Right now, you have a choice to make. Now choose quickly."

Thyra looked around at the dark elves, held captive by the well-armed, enhanced light elves. They struggled against their captors, but they were fruitless efforts.

"Decide quickly, girl," said Volund. "Or I will decide for you. I'm not afraid of death, but I will make you regret me having to put my life on the line."

"An impossible decision," said Hillevi, having overheard the conversation between Thyra and Volund.

"What do we do?" said Jarl.

She looked around at the light elves who had captured her fellow dark elves.

"There are too many of them," said Jarl. "Hakon and Saga, our two finest, have been captured already."

"I'm aware," said Hillevi frustrated at Jarl for stating the obvious.

"Then what do we do?"

"I'm going to do something," said Holgor.

"What?"

"I'll distract him so she can take him down quickly."

"That's suicide."

"There's nothing else that can be done."

"I'll do it," said Ove.

"Think about your son," said Holgor.

"I gave the Valkyries the key. Let me make up for that."

There was a pause from Holgor then he said, "I won't let you do that."

"I don't need your permission."

And Ove hit Holgor in the back of his head with all his might. The light elf stumbled and fell to the ground unconscious.

"Be safe, my friend," he whispered.

Ove looked out at Volund, took a deep breath, and emerged from his hiding place. Volund noticed the attention shift of his light elves and turned to face where they were looking.

"Ove," he said.

"Volund," said Ove.

Volund's expression of surprise quickly turned to anger as Ove approached.

"So, you're with the dark elves? A traitor to your own kind."

"I've betrayed no one."

"Have you forgotten already what happened to your family? How I peeled their flesh from their bones. Your son will suffer far worse now."

"You'll do nothing to him," said Ove.

"And why is that?"

"Because you'll be dead," said Ove.

Volund smirked.

"Is that so?"

Ove nodded.

"And who is . . ."

Volund could not finish his statement. A wave of red energy washed over him, bringing him to his knees. Ove pivoted and started to run.

"Kill . . . them . . . all," managed Volund.

Volund caught Ove from the back with a single strike of his spear. Without relenting her power, Thyra ran up to Volund, stripped the weapon from his hands, and tossed it aside.

"Yield," she said.

"Never," he said.

She grabbed him by the back of his neck.

"Yield," she shouted.

"I'm prepared . . . to die . . . are they?"

Thyra looked at the dark elves being held at the blade of a sword and let up on her attack. Volund massaged the back of his neck and stood up. He put his hand up so his men would stop.

Ove pulled himself through the dirt, bleeding profusely from the gash in his back. As he did so, Holgor regained consciousness and saw his friend struggling to retreat.

"No," he said and ran out to grab him.

"You, too," said Volund.

Holgor did not respond but grabbed Ove and pulled him to safety.

"I will go with you," said Thyra.

Volund smiled the largest smile he could muster.

"Men. Let them go," said Volund.

"But you have to promise to defeat Hildr and Svipul, too."

"Of course,"

"Thyra, don't do it," shouted Helga, who appeared in the town's gateway, having recovered from Gunnhild's attack.

"I've made my decision."

"There is another way," said Hakon, being held up by Saga.

"We all fight together," said Saga.

"I will help," said Holgor unsheathing his sword.

"Me too," said Hillevi.

"I guess I'm in also," said Jarl.

At that moment, the dark elves who had fled started pouring back into the town from the tunnels underground, outnumbering the light elves two to one.

"This is our town and our realm," said Hakon attempting to stand on his own. "And these are our people, and no one is going anywhere today."

"You will soon find out that you are wrong about that," said Volund.

Not since the light elves first attacked two centuries prior had a battle been waged in Svartalfheim like that which was happening against Volund and his villainous soldiers. His men were clearly well-trained warriors, and Volund himself was an incredibly skilled alchemist and fighter. Light elf against dark elf resulted in casualties on both sides. Men and women were dropping quickly, and lives were needlessly lost for one man's selfish goals. Buildings burned, and the ground was scarred.

Thyra, though a novice warrior compared to Volund, was a natural alchemist, and the dark elves had spent the past two hundred years training for a second fight with the light elves. Swords clashed, and blood spilled.

The realm of Svartalfheim shook with incredible ferocity. At first, it was not clear how things would resolve themselves. Thyra was naturally gifted, but Volund had years of training. The dark elves were disciplined warriors, but the light elves were enhanced. The dark elves were on their home turf, but the light elves had the numbers. However, as the fighting continued, it became clear that Thyra and the dark elves were winning. Volund could not keep up, despite his best efforts, and his minions were being beaten back one by one.

Thyra's red energy flowed over Volund, bringing him to his knees. His armor shifted as Thyra attempted to transmute it into something more malleable. He put his hand up to block, but it was a fruitless effort.

"Yield," shouted Thyra.

"Never," shouted Volund.

The armor started to melt.

"Give up," Thyra shouted.

Feeling his power slipping, Volund nodded.

"Ok, ok," he said.

Thyra pulled back.

"I will let your men return to Alfheim, but you—"

"What? Are you going to kill me?" You don't have what it takes."

"I . . ."

Thyra concentrated her red aura into the palm of her hand.

"As I suspected. All bark. Your parents were at least killers. They had what it took. You, you're nothing. But if I can't have your power, neither can you."

He spun and threw two daggers in her direction. She quickly dodged right and blasted him with all her might. He crashed to the ground and was quickly stabbed through the heart by a nearby dark elf warrior.

"No," shouted Saga, running past Thyra.

Thyra turned around to see the two daggers had landed in Hakon and Hillevi.

Volund laughed as best he could as he bled out.

"See you . . . around," he mumbled.

Thyra confirmed he was dead and then ran over to Hillevi and Hakon. The fighting had paused as the light elves all waited to see what would happen next, and the dark elves were not eager to reengage.

The daggers each pierced their pelts.

"Is there anything we can do?" said Saga in a panic.

Hakon grabbed Hillevi's hand. She turned and looked at him as the life faded from her face. He looked at her.

"It's ok," he said.

"Brother," said Saga.

Jarl spied what happened and ran over. He knelt by his sister. Tears were running down his face.

"Live. With. Purpose," whispered Hillevi.

"Protect . . . our people," said Hakon.

And with that, the two were gone. Saga and Jarl rested their hands upon their brother and sister and cried.

Thyra felt the pain of their loss, but her attention, as was everyone else's, was quickly drawn to the center of town where yet another Bifrost bridge touched down. When it was gone, standing over Volund's body were Hildr, Svipul, and Gunnhild. Drawn all over Hildr and Svipul's bodies were elaborate runic markings. Gunnhild stepped forward and inspected Volund.

"Light elves," announced Hildr. "Your master is dead, but you are not yet free. My sister and I need ten dark elves. Alive. Once we have them, you will be free of Volund. Free of us. If you refuse, we will make Volund look like a loving parent. Do you all understand?"

"We refuse," shouted Holgor.

Hildr looked his way and flapped her massive wings, propelling her towards him. He stepped backward, shaken by how quickly she moved. Hildr grabbed his head, and he batted her forearms to get free, but it was to no avail.

"Pay close attention to your friend here," shouted Hildr.

She pressed her thumbs to Holgor's eyes. He screamed as she blinded him; blood poured over her hands. He thrashed about, but she pressed on his skull and, with ease, crushed it. His body went limp immediately, and she dropped him.

"I am tired," she said. "Now do as I say."

The dark elves, who had been fighting the light elves, quickly took up arms. The pause in battle was over.

Thyra grabbed Saga and Jarl by the arm and pulled them to their feet. "Get everyone you can out of here. I'll handle them," she said.

"Can you?" said Jarl.

"I'll help her," said Helga.

"No. You go with them, Helga. I have a plan."

"I can't leave you here."

"You'll be a distraction."

"But . . ."

"Go."

Saga grabbed Helga by the arm.

"I'm your flygja. I'm supposed to protect you."

"You did. You helped me realize I was not alone when it felt like I had no one."

Helga sighed and nodded. She turned to run with Saga and Jarl.

Thyra turned towards Hildr, Svipul, and Gunnhild.

"You at least avenged your parents," said Hildr gesturing back towards Volund.

Then without hesitation, the two Valkyries charged Thyra from opposing directions. Thyra unleashed her power on them, but they dodged the attack. Quickly they were upon her. They were fast. Thyra decided to evade at the last minute, and they barely missed. Thyra attempted to counter, but Hildr and Svipul had already adjusted their approach. Hildr went high and Svipul went low. Thyra would have to choose. She opted for Svipul. That was a mistake. Hildr unsheathed her sword as she neared. Svipul ate Thyra's attack, but only to distract her long enough for a killing blow from Hildr. Thyra realized what had happened just in time and again lept backward to evade. The swing of Hildr's blade missed Thyra's nose by a quarter of an inch.

"You won't be able to keep that up," said Hildr.

Helga led Saga and Jarl to Ratatoskr, who was still waiting, despite the commotion.

"I expected you to flee," said Helga.

"I thought about it."

"I'm glad you didn't."

"What's going on in there?" said Ratatoskr.

"Volund is dead, but the Valkyries returned, and they're far more powerful than they should be," said Helga. "Thyra is facing them, but . . ."

"It doesn't look good?"

"I don't know."

"And they've commanded the remaining light elves to round up ten dark elves," added Saga. "Once they do, the Valkyries will surely disengage Thyra and take their captors with them."

"Ratatoskr, how many people can you take at once?" said Helga.

"As long as they're touching, the sky is the limit."

"Ok," said Helga looking back at the town. "I have an idea."

Thyra channeled everything she could muster into the palms of her hands and unleashed a wave of energy that sent Hildr and Svipul flying, but they bounced back quickly and kept up the assault.

And yet the most your father could ever do was fire blasts of energy much like it seems you will only ever do, she thought, remembering the words of Volund.

"Come on; you can do better than this," she said to herself.

Thyra spied a broken sword to her right. She leaped for it and, in a quick, fluid motion, grabbed it and transformed it into a perfect replica of Gambanteinn, which she lost hours earlier in Alfheim. She deflected multiple sword strikes by Hildr and Svipul and barely avoided another killing blow that caught her left cheek. Blood dripped onto her pelt as she retreated.

Gunnhild watched the battle between the two Valkyries and Thyra with utter fascination. She was stunned by how powerful her work made the Valkyries, but she was even more enamored by the natural alchemical abilities of Thyra. She could understand Volund's obsession. If she could master that power, she could do whatever she wanted.

"It's a waste if they kill her," she whispered.

Gunnhild pulled the rune stone from her pouch that brought down lightning bolts.

"But if I can stun her . . ."

Thyra swung the Gambanteinn replica at Hildr and Svipul. They parried her attack, but she countered. Sparks flew from the fast and powerful swordplay.

Gunnhild watched patiently from the sideline, and when a moment presented itself, she triggered her runestone. But Thyra was one step ahead. She raised her sword above her head and turned her right palm towards Svipul. The lightning channeled through the blade, mixed with her red aura, and tore through Svipul, sending her tumbling across the battlefield. She crashed to a stop inside a dark elf home that collapsed on top of her.

"Do not help," shouted Hildr at Gunnhild.

Gunnhild dropped the rune and put her hands up.

"Sorry."

Helga picked up Ratatoskr and made for the town's front gate with Saga and Jarl behind her. They snuck inside and, for a moment, gazed upon the chaos. Thyra was busy fighting the two Valkyries, which was an impressive display of ferocity. Meanwhile, the light elves were busy trying to round up the dark elves, but the dark elves were not going down easily.

"There." Helga pointed to a building on the other side of the battlefield. "That's where they're taking the captured."

"Here we go," said Ratatoskr.

The Bifrost touched down around them and they were inside the home a moment later. Nine dark elves were already tied up and squirming to get free. "

"Grab them," shouted Helga.

Jarl and Saga each put a hand on one of the nine.

"All right, Ratatoskr, do your—" Helga couldn't finish.

The home door slammed open, and in the doorway was Gunnhild. Using a runic fire stone, she cast fire at Helga. Ratatoskr leaped from her hold onto the nine dark elves.

"Go without me," she said.

"Planned on it," said Ratatoskr and triggered the Bifrost bridge.

In a second, all that remained was Gunnhild and Helga.

"I let you go before. I won't do it again," said Gunnhild.

"We have to go back," said Saga.

"No way," said Ratatoskr. "You two go if you want, but I'm done. I keep risking my neck for all of you; this isn't even my battle. Consider my debt paid to Thyra with interest."

With that, he triggered the Bifrost and was gone.

"What do we do?" said Jarl.

"What can we do? It's in Thyra's hands now."

THIRTY-THREE

ONLY HUMAN

Moments Before Ratatoskr Left

The Bifrost touching down over the dark elf where the captives were stored drew the attention of Thyra, Hildr, and Svipul.

She gestured at Gunnhild to go check it out.

"You are only making this harder on yourselves," said Hildr to Thyra.

"The same could be said for you. All this chaos and destruction for what? Do you even know what you're fighting for anymore?"

Svipul looked at her sister for an answer.

"I have been a tool my entire life, but that ends today," answered Hildr. "If that means your people have to make some sacrifices, then so be it. The gods will use me no more."

"You think you're better than us, that your cause has meaning; therefore, your actions are justified, but you're no better than Odin. You're no better than Thor. You're no better than Volund."

"The only thing you have that's real in the nine realms is your own personal strength."

"Stop," shouted Svipul. "She is right. Look at what we've done."

"Not you too," said Hildr.

"We can't keep doing this. We are the problem. We have caused all this destruction. Not anyone else. We have."

"Sister, if you are not with me, then you are my enemy as well."

212

"Then I am your enemy, sister. I should have sided with Gunnr before, but it is not too late to change. Hildr, you have—"

Hildr caught her across the neck with the tip of her sword, cutting her throat so deep that, at first, Svipul could not feel a thing; she could only cease to talk.

"No," whispered Thyra.

Svipul dropped her sword and put her hands to her neck as blood seeped over her fingers. She stumbled backward and fell to one knee. She had a stunned look spread across her face—a mix of terror and surprise.

"Sister," shouted Hildr.

She moved for her, but Svipul put up one of her bloodied hands, telling her not to come closer. Hildr paused.

Thyra observed the life drain from Svipul. She quickly shifted her focus to Hildr, whose eyes had turned red with anger and sadness. At that moment, the home where Gunnhild had found Helga erupted in flames, and the rune writer and flygja burst through the door into the open, fighting one another.

"My sisters are all gone," whispered Hildr, Helga and Gunnhild's distraction breaking her trance-like state.

"Stop this now," said Thyra.

Hildr shifted her attention away from Svipul towards Thyra.

"I . . . have nothing. And soon, so will you. When I'm done with you, I'll find every dark elf living in Midgard, deliver them to human settlements, and let the savages have their way. You know what fear does to their kind," said Hildr.

"It's not too late for you to stop this madness," said Thyra.

"And then I'll visit Hel to ensure Calder suffers properly."

"Shut your mouth."

"You had to intervene, and you'll learn there is a cost for doing so."

"Shut. Your. Mouth," shouted Thyra.

"I'll tell Calder that everything he must suffer in the afterlife is because his daughter could not just step aside."

"Enough," Thyra shouted before tackling Hildr to the ground.

They rolled around in the dirt, and Thyra landed punch after punch on Hildr's face. The tattoos faded on Hildr's body, and she could not defend herself.

Thyra straddled Hildr, restricting her movement, and raised the Gambanteinn replica over Hildr's head.

"Do it," said Hildr. "I have nothing to live for anyway."

Gunnhild and Helga had stopped their battle. The dark elves and the light elves had stopped theirs as well. Fires burned, and smoke plumes went skyward, but not a sound was made other than the crackling of embers.

Thyra held the sword's hilt so tightly that her knuckles turned white.

"You took from me so much," said Thyra.

"Thyra," Helga said.

She looked at her flygja and let out a deep sigh. Thyra threw the sword to the ground, and her red aura encompassed her entire body. She put her hands to either side of Hildr's head. The red aura glowed so brightly that Helga and Gunnhild shielded their eyes. But the red eventually faded, and in its place, a golden hue shone over the town.

"It's beautiful," whispered Helga and Gunnhild in unison.

"You let fear and anger control you. But I will not let it control me."

The golden glow flowed from Thyra's body, over Hildr's, from her head to her feet, wrapping her in a warm cocoon. The injuries she had sustained during the battle healed, and the red in her eyes from tears disappeared.

When she was back to normal, Thyra let go and stood up.

"You healed me?" said Hildr looking at the front and back of her hands. "That was a mistake."

Hildr jumped to her feet and lunged for Thyra. She hit Thyra in the face, but Thyra did not budge. Hildr's hand just throbbed.

"What is this? What did you do to do me?"

"Humans used to frighten me. But they no longer do. That is why I turned you into one," said Thyra.

"You did what?" said Hildr.

She tried sprouting her Valkyrie wings, but nothing happened.

"This can't be."

"My father said an altercation does not have to end in death. Be grateful I did not kill you," said Thyra as she rested a hand on Hildr's shoulder.

Hildr fell to her knees and dropped her face to her chest. A nearby dark elf ran over to her, pulled her hands behind her back, and tied them together. Hildr did not resist.

"Light elves lay down your weapons," shouted Thyra.

Right then, the clinking sound of swords dropping carried over the town.

THIRTY-FOUR

A CHILD IS OWED JUSTICE

"You hear that?" said Saga.

Jarl nodded.

Jarl and Saga, along with the nine freed dark elves, ran into the town to see Thyra and Helga standing over a bound Gunnhild and Hildr. The light elves were making their way into the center of town. Thyra had in her hand the Bifrost keys that Volund and Hildr each used to get to Svartalfheim.

"Join hands," said Helga to the light elves.

Reluctantly at first, but eventually, they all did as instructed.

"I'll be back shortly," said Thyra.

She grabbed the light elf nearest her and triggered one of the Bifrost keys. The rainbow bridge touched down, and Thyra and all the surviving light elves disappeared. She returned moments later.

"I took them back to Alfheim," she said to Saga and Jarl. "With Volund gone, they can chart their own course."

"What about these two?" said Saga looking at Hildr and Gunnhild.

"The rune writer was conscripted into their service," said Thyra.

"But she isn't to be trusted," said Helga.

"And now she is the more dangerous of the two," said Thyra.

"Let me go. I promise to leave you all alone."

"Don't trust her," said Helga.

"Let her speak," said Thyra.

"The Valkyries saved me from my death so that I could help them, and I admit to getting a bit caught up in their plan, but all I really want is to return to my husband."

"And where is he?" said Thyra.

"Somewhere in the Midgardian Sea off the coast of Borgarnes. If you drop me there, I will find him."

"Thyra, do not trust her," said Helga.

"What do you want to do with her?" said Thyra.

"I don't know. Can't you transmute away her powers too?"

"Her powers are learned. It is different. We should let her return to her husband."

"I don't think that is a good idea."

"Gunnhild, I will let you return to your husband," said Thyra.

Helga shook her head.

"You, however, Hildr. You are not free to go."

She did not bother looking up when Thyra spoke to her.

"We'll put her to work," said Saga. "Valkyries have extensive knowledge of the nine realms, and we still have not reclaimed all the texts lost during the Great War."

"What about you?" said Jarl. "You are welcome to stay here in Svartalfheim. Leave Midgard behind."

Thyra looked around at the town and the dark elves that inhabited it.

"I have long wished to come here for a sense of belonging. But Mimir said something I cannot ignore."

"What?" Jarl said. "And who is Mimir?"

"Mimir is the wisest man alive, or so he says. But he told me that I am not the only dark elf in Midgard. Others are out there, and they need to know Svartalfheim is rebuilding—that they are not alone."

"Thyra, can I talk to you for a moment?" said Helga. "Privately."

Thyra nodded and followed Helga around the corner, away from Saga and Jarl.

"I owe you my life," she said. "I was born of you, and we still share part of a mind, and our fates are still intertwined, but when we first met, I said you and I will drift apart since we are not one. Do you remember this?"

"I do."

"I'm afraid that drifting is happening faster than I suspected. I think I need to find my own way, even if it's only temporary. I need to know who I am."

Thyra got on one knee and put a hand on Helga's shoulder.

"I would not want it any other way. Thank you for being there when I hit my lowest. Where do you want me to take you?"

"You can leave me in Borgarnes as well, and I will figure things out from there."

Thyra left Gunnhild and Helga in Borgarnes before departing for Mímisbrunnr. The rainbow bridge made Mimir perk up.

"Hello?" he said.

"It's me, Thyra," said Thyra stepping from the dissipating rainbow.

"So, you were successful?" said Mimir.

"We stopped the Valkyries," said Thyra.

"Good."

"I came to ask you something, though," said Thyra.

"You want to know where to find the other dark elves?"

Thyra nodded.

"They're scattered around Midgard and actively living in seclusion. Finding them will not be easy. That's if they even want to be found."

"Not all do, I'm sure, but those that feel alone and disconnected are who I'm trying to reach."

"And I can help you with that," said Mimir.

"One other thing. I have come into the possession of a second Bifrost, and these things seem too dangerous to be out in the wild. I was hoping . . ."

"That you could leave one with me? Yes, you may."

"Since only those directed here may reach you, I thought it would limit the number of people with access to it."

"Place it on the ground in front of me," said Mimir.

Thyra did as instructed, and a golden beam of light shone from Mimir's eye over the Bifrost key. It disappeared shortly after.

"Thank you," said Thyra.